Quest
–for the–
Lost Prince

Dave & Neta Jackson

Illustrated by Julian Jackson

BETHANY HOUSE PUBLISHERS
MINNEAPOLIS, MINNESOTA 55438

Inside illustration by Julian Jackson.
Cover illustration by Catherine Reishus McLaughlin.

All scripture quotations are from the King James Version of the Bible.

Published by Bethany House Publishers
A Ministry of Bethany Fellowship, Inc.
11300 Hampshire Ave. South
Minneapolis, Minnesota 55438

Library of Congress Cataloging-in-Publication Data

Jackson, Dave.
    Quest for the lost prince / Dave and Neta Jackson.
        p.   cm. — (Trailblazer books)
    Summary: Jova, a seven-year-old Kru boy in Liberia and a captive slave of his people's enemy the Grebos, witnesses the dramatic conversion to Christianity of the Kru prince Kaboo and his subsequent disappearance; seven years later, in 1893, Jova sails to America to find Prince Kaboo and bring him back to rule his people.
    1. Morris, Samuel, 1873–1893—Juvenile fiction. [1. Morris, Samuel, 1873–1893—Fiction. 2. Kru (African people)—Fiction. 3. Grebo (African people)—Fiction. 4. Liberia—Fiction. 5. Blacks—Liberia—Fiction. 6. Missionaries—Fiction. 7. Christian life—Fiction.] I. Jackson, Neta. II. Title. III. Series: Jackson, Dave.
    Trailblazer books.
PZ7.J13248Qu   1996
[Fic]—dc20   96–9941
ISBN 1–55661–472–1   CIP
                                                                  AC

As amazing as it is, all the information in this story about Prince Kaboo (later called Samuel Morris) is true. In several respects, the character of Jova coincides with that of a Kru boy who was given the Christian name of Henry O'Neil or Henry O. Neil. As a slave of the Grebos at the same time as Kaboo's imprisonment, he witnessed Kaboo's final torture, the flash, the voice from heaven, and Kaboo's mysterious escape. Henry also escaped at the same time and found his way to Monrovia, where he confirmed Kaboo's story, became a Christian, and was baptized.

Later, Samuel Morris (Prince Kaboo) arranged for Henry to come to the United States to be educated. The real Henry O'Neil did not, however, wait six years before going to Monrovia, or make the journey as a quest to bring Kaboo back to the throne. The assassins and the final meeting between Kaboo and Jova are fictional. But Samuel Morris's witness did inspire many to become missionaries to Africa and elsewhere.

DAVE AND NETA JACKSON are a husband/wife writing team who have authored or coauthored many books on marriage and family, the church, and relationships, including the books accompanying the Secret Adventures video series, the Pet Parables series, and the Caring Parent series.

They have three children: Julian, the illustrator for the Trailblazer series, Rachel, their married daughter, and Samantha, their Cambodian foster daughter. They make their home in Evanston, Illinois, where they are active members of Reba Place Church.

CONTENTS

Chapter 1

The King's Ransom

FOURTEEN-YEAR-OLD JOVA gathered with the other Kru people in the village square in front of the king's great house. He lifted first one bare foot and then the other to get relief from the burning heat of the packed earth. It was a particularly hot day, and the silvery sun high overhead drew beads of sweat from his dark forehead.

There was a rustling in the leaves of the soap trees that towered above the thatched roof of the king's house as two monkeys jumped from limb to limb. *I wouldn't mind being a monkey sometimes*, Jova thought. *All they do is play up there where the cool breezes blow.*

Just then, the reed mat moved aside from the door on the king's house, and two servants came out onto the porch carrying ostrich-feather fans. Jova stood as tall as he could, nearly as tall as the men around him. This was no time for playing like a monkey; he wanted to be counted among the warriors. Jova had a strong, handsome face with large, clear eyes that did not shy from looking others in the eye. He kept his close-cropped hair neatly free from nappy tangles.

Jova had already gone through the dreaded "bush-devil" initiation school. Supposedly it had made a man of him, so now he must act like one. He waited quietly for the king to come out and speak.

Everyone waited, but the king did not appear.

While Jova watched the door of the king's house, he thought about the bush-devil school. Around the age of twelve, every boy in the village was taken out into the jungle to a fenced-in stockade made of tightly woven palm fronds and thorn branches. It was impossible to escape. There, for many months, a "devil" taught the boys the customs of the Kru people and how to be a man, even the art of war. It had been a terrifying experience for Jova. Sometimes, he thought the figure that looked like a walking bush was a man in a bushlike costume, but other times Jova believed that he was indeed a devil. Whatever he was, he had remarkable, magical powers enabling him to hypnotize a chicken, cause a tree to die, or put a curse on an enemy.

Jova's hand drifted to his forehead, where a small

blue tattoo and scar extended from between his eyebrows down to the bridge of his nose. It was the Kru tribal mark and proved that he had gone through the bush-devil school. When he and his friends had finally graduated, they had been permitted to come home, where a great celebration awaited them. All of Jova's relatives had honored him. His father, of course, was not there. He had been killed in the last war. But his mother, uncle, and aunts had made a magnificent feast.

However, in spite of the initiation, Jova knew that he would not really be accepted as a man among his people until he proved himself with some heroic deed—maybe killing a leopard or fighting bravely in battle or bringing back some treasure to his people— the honey from a hive of bees, an elephant tusk, or some iron for knives and spears.

A fly buzzing around Jova's head brought his mind back to the present. He brushed it away with the back of his hand, and then noticed the reed mat on the king's door move.

When the king finally emerged from the dark interior of his mud-walled house, he did not walk proudly in his flowing brown-and-white striped robe. Instead, four of his personal guards carried him out on a wooden chair. As soon as they set him down, the two servants stepped forward to wave their ostrich-feather fans to cool him.

When the people saw their king, they gasped. His head hung slightly to one side, and his eyelids drooped until they nearly closed over bloodshot, watery eyes. His kinky gray hair was matted and dull. It was obvious that the old man was very sick.

When the murmuring finally became silent, the king spoke in a breathy, weak voice. "My people," he

said, and then coughed as he drew in another breath. "I am dying."

The men shuffled nervously, and some women around the edge of the group began a moan that rose to the high-pitched trill of grief. But when the king held out a thin, shaky arm from which leathery folds of skin hung like rags, silence returned.

"You must not grieve for me," he said. "There will be time enough for that later. Pray now that when I die you will have no cause to grieve for yourselves."

He wheezed again, trying to catch his breath, and a whisper skittered among the people as they turned from one to another asking what he meant. The king was quick to explain. "When I die, there will be no one to take my place, and without a strong king on the throne, our enemies—the bloodthirsty Grebos—will see our weakness, and they are likely to attack us again."

Another murmur went through the crowd. Memories of long, vicious battles, of lost brothers and fathers, of burned crops and destroyed houses, and women and children taken captive were still fresh in the minds of all the Kru people. For they had suffered a bitter defeat at the hands of the cruel Grebos only a few years before.

The Kru people could not survive another war. They were just beginning to recover from the last one. As the king's dreadful words began to sink in, the high-pitched trilling wail of some of the women could again be heard around the edge of the crowd.

Finally, the old man raised his hand once more to

Finally, the old man raised his hand once more to call for quiet. Then he continued, "There is only one hope. My son, Kaboo, must be found and brought back to rule in my place. Without him, we are doomed. But with a new young king on the throne, we would be safe because the Grebos would know we are strong."

A coughing fit silenced the king, and the crowd held its breath until the spasm stopped. The king sat with his eyes closed as he gulped in air like a fish out of water. When he seemed out of danger, quiet whispering spread among the Kru people.

It had been six years since there had been any news of Prince Kaboo, and most people considered him dead. But there had been reports that he had escaped safely from his Grebo captors and had fled into the forest. Many doubted it, and even those who believed the story had given up hope of him returning safely. Probably, they speculated, he had been attacked by the fierce "leopard men," those cannibals who roamed the jungle at night killing and eating fellow humans who ventured too far away from their village in the dark. Or maybe he had been bitten by a poisonous snake, or pulled into a river by a giant crocodile. Anything could have happened; the jungle was a dangerous place. So, whether he had not escaped, or had escaped but met tragedy in the jungle, most people believed Prince Kaboo was dead.

But the king believed otherwise. His confidence that his son was alive set everyone talking. Where could Kaboo be? How could anyone find him this long after he had disappeared?

"Silence!" shouted one of the king's guards. "Your king addresses you."

"My good people," continued the king when quiet had returned, "to the brave warrior who finds and returns Prince Kaboo to sit on this throne, I offer a king's ransom—five balls of rubber the size of a man's head, twenty goats and twenty pigs, four elephant tusks as tall as a man, plus all the rice one man can haul in a day." He wheezed a great breath and then said, "Only find my son! Find my son!" And he raised both hands as though giving his tribe a blessing.

With that the king's guards carried him back into his house, and the people broke into an uproar of cheers, arguments, and general confusion as they speculated on whether Prince Kaboo was dead or alive and whether anyone could find him.

"Such a fortune!" said a muscular warrior standing near Jova. "Anyone who wins a king's ransom would be the richest man in the village."

"How can the king offer that much wealth?" said another. "I know he has that many goats and pigs, and maybe he has the rice. But the rubber and the elephant tusks—they must be hidden somewhere. I've never seen them."

"If the Grebos hear he has rubber and ivory, they will attack us for that alone, king or no king," said the first man.

"I don't think the prince is alive. How could he be after this long?"

But Jova did not cheer, or argue, or talk to anyone. His mind was racing. He would go on a quest that everyone would consider brave. He would prove he was a man. He would bring home to his people a great treasure and get a king's ransom in return.

These thoughts raced through Jova's mind because . . . he knew where Kaboo had gone, and, as far as he could tell, he was the only person who knew!

Chapter 2

A Prince at Pawn

IT HAD HAPPENED SIX YEARS before when Jova was only seven, but he had seen it all . . .

Day after day, the Grebo warriors had attacked their village. Brave Kru men had fought them off, several falling under the spears of the Grebo warriors. Their small fields of rice and sugarcane around the village were burned; the only crop that survived was the roots of the cassava plant. All the goats, pigs, and chickens had been scared into the jungle, and the village was low on food.

One day when it seemed that the Grebos had withdrawn, Jova's father and several other men went hunting for food. Possibly they would come across some of their livestock roaming in the forest, or maybe they could find some other food—small game or edible roots and tubers.

But they never came back. The little expedition was attacked at the river when they were out in the water checking their traps.

The next day, while the Kru village was having a funeral for the men of the food expedition, the Grebos attacked again. This time guards were not on duty, and the Grebos ran through the village burning houses and capturing women and children before the remaining men could mount a defense. That raid was the beginning of the end. There had been so much death and destruction that the people felt like giving up.

For as long as anyone could remember, there had been trouble between the Krus and the Grebos. It had usually amounted to brief raids on each others' villages. Sometimes, it involved the "leopard men" from one tribe or the other who caught an enemy tribal member alone in the forest at night. But these disputes usually ended when "sufficient" revenge had been taken, and there would be a year or two of peace before another incident broke out. It was like an ongoing feud.

But this time the Grebos were waging an all-out war on the Kru. "Maybe we should just surrender," suggested some of the Kru elders to their king that night around the fire. "Surrender certainly can't be worse than this destruction. Soon there will be nothing left of us."

But the proud king resisted. To him, it was hard

to think of anything worse than surrender. It might even mean his death. He just shook his head and walked slowly back to his house.

The next morning, just as the light began to turn the sky from a deep violet to greenish gray, terrible screams broke out from the jungle all around the village. Seven-year-old Jova peeked outside in time to see hundreds of Grebo warriors running between the houses. He was just pulling back when strong arms grabbed him and pulled him out. He fought to free himself, but the powerful warrior tripped Jova, then sat on him while he tied his hands and feet with cords. Then he picked the boy up and carried him like a sack of rice over his shoulder.

Jova kicked and squirmed until he almost made the man lose his balance. Angry and yelling at his uncooperative captive, the Grebo threw Jova to the ground and hit Jova so hard that all the breath was knocked out of him. The boy lay stunned as he stared up into his captor's face.

Three parallel lines on the man's right cheek marked him as Grebo. His nostrils flared, and his eyes flashed. "Be still, or I will crush you!"

The words sounded strange with their thick, Grebo accent, but Jova understood them because both the Grebos and the Krus used the Kruan language.

The blow and the warning were enough of a shock that when the Grebo picked him up again, Jova did not kick and struggle but allowed the man to carry him into the jungle.

When they arrived at a small clearing a mile or so from the Kru village, the Grebo warrior put him down alongside other prisoners. The captives were herded into a small group surrounded by a few warriors, all of whom wore the three-lined tribal mark on their right cheeks. Their ready spears prevented any escape. After a whispered consultation, the Grebos cut the cords that bound the prisoners' feet and forced them to walk ahead of them down the narrow trail.

They marched for a day and a half until they came to the main Grebo village. There the prisoners were shoved into a stockade and guarded day and night.

As the Kru prisoners watched and listened from behind the prison fence, it became clear why the Grebos had been attacking them so fiercely. They had a new war chief who had decided that the way to end the ongoing feud with the Kru was to wipe them out completely—or at least reduce them to such a weak nation that they would never rise again.

A few days later, young Jova and the other Krus were drawn to the wall of their stockade by a great commotion outside. From all the noise, Jova thought another large group of prisoners must be arriving. But when he looked through the closely spaced bamboo poles that formed his prison, he saw only three captives; two women and . . . Prince Kaboo, the king's fourteen-year-old son!

The Grebos were dancing around the prince and yelling that the war was over. The Kru people had been defeated.

Within the stockade, the prisoners began talking

among themselves, wondering what it all meant. Would they be allowed to go home?

When Prince Kaboo and the two women were thrown into the stockade, the other prisoners ran to their aid, but their attention was mainly on the young prince. They picked him up from the dust where he had fallen, brushed the dirt off him and offered him what little water they'd been given.

"What has happened to our village?" cried first one voice, then another. Slowly, the story came out as Prince Kaboo and the two frightened women helped one another tell the tale.

The last battle had overrun the town. Those who had not been captured or killed had fled into the jungle. This time, *all* the remaining houses had been burned. Everything of value was stolen, and still the Grebo chased the fleeing Kru people, killing anyone they caught. Finally, to end the slaughter, the king sent a messenger to the Grebo war chief offering a full surrender.

The Grebos agreed to stop chasing and killing the Krus if the king and all his people would return to the site of their former village and surrender in person.

The next morning, the Kru people came out of the jungle in twos and threes to stand among the smoldering ruins of their houses and give themselves up to the Grebo war chief and his army of fierce warriors. They were a sad remnant—dirty, exhausted, and weeping. Many were wounded.

In exchange for their lives, the Grebo war chief said that each year the Kru people would have to pay a tax of twenty baskets of rice, fifty cassava roots, ten bundles of sugarcane, and ten goats. Furthermore, the first payment was due immediately.

"But," protested the Kru king, "you have destroyed everything. We cannot possibly pay such a big tax."

"Either pay the tax or die." The war chief shrugged as though he did not care what they chose.

"Give us time," begged the king, "and we will pay all you ask."

"How do I know this? Maybe you will all run away into the jungle. Or maybe you'll try to regain your strength and wage a war of revenge on us," objected the war chief. "Isn't that what has happened for years?"

"*Us* take revenge?" said the Kru king angrily. "It is you who always start something new."

"Silence! We are the victors, and you are worth nothing more than a chicken feather blown by the breeze. You will do as I say!"

Remembering his circumstance, the king bowed and said humbly, "Then I give you my word. We will not retaliate. We will pay your tax—only give us time."

"You are our slaves now," sneered the war chief. "Your word means nothing. Give us something in pawn to prove that you will pay your tax. Then we will spare your lives. When you pay your debt, we will return your pawn."

The king looked hopelessly around at the ruins of his town. "I have nothing left," he said.

"Who is that beside you?" said the war chief, pointing to the handsome boy standing beside the king. It was Kaboo.

"Oh! Just a lowly boy of the village," said the king, hoping to protect his son.

"Do not try to fool us, you dog!" spat the war chief. "We can see that he wears a gold ring. He must be your son."

"No, no. He is just a worthless village boy." This time the king pushed Kaboo away from him so hard that the boy tripped and fell into the ashes of a nearby house.

"Worthless, is he?" said the war chief. "Then bring him here, and I shall kill him this instant." He raised his machete as he nodded to one of his warriors.

"Have mercy!" pleaded the king. "You are right. He is my son. Only do not harm him."

The war chief looked scornfully at the Kru king groveling before him. "Yes, I think you do value him. We will take him in pawn. When you pay your tax debt, you may have him back."

With that, the Grebo warriors had left the burned-out Kru town and brought away Prince Kaboo as their prisoner.

24

Within a week, most of the Kru captives were distributed among various Grebo families as slaves. Seven-year-old Jova went to live with one of the elders of the village who had four wives. Each of the wives and even the family's children had the authority to boss him around from dawn to dark: "Fetch some wood for the fire." "Clean up this mess!" "What are you standing there for? I need some water. Hurry up!"

He had never worked so hard in all his life. There was not a moment to rest, let alone play. He looked for a chance to escape, but someone was always watching him. And even if Jova had gotten away from the elder's wives, whom he called the "fearsome foursome," he was in a village with hundreds of Grebo around, all of whom knew he was a slave.

One day when Jova was going to fetch water from the stream that ran through the center of the village, he heard a jangling sound coming from within the stockade prison where he and the other captives had been held. He looked through the narrow gaps between the bamboo poles and was shocked to see Prince Kaboo making his way across the small enclosure. The noise came from a log that was attached to the older boy's foot. The log was about two feet long and was as large as a man's leg. On one side of the log, at about the halfway point, a deep notch had been cut, large enough to fit around Kaboo's ankle. Then an iron strap had been nailed across the open side to keep his leg within the notch.

A chain was attached to each end of the log. It

was long enough to create a loop that served as a handle. By lifting the log by the chain, Kaboo could support it so it didn't drag on the ground or trip his other foot. Jova watched in horror as Kaboo made a great effort to swing his logged leg forward to take one faltering step. Jova could see that despite the lifting chain, the heavy hobble had gouged sores into Kaboo's ankle.

Walking was slow going, and obviously painful.

"Kaboo," called Jova softly. "Prince Kaboo."

The prince looked over toward the fence. When he finally spotted Jova's dark eyes, he looked around frantically to see if anyone was watching, then waved furtively with his other hand. "Go away," whispered Kaboo just loudly enough to be heard across the yard. "You will be caught."

"Why are you still here? Why haven't they made you a slave to some family?" asked Jova, ignoring the warning.

Kaboo made a few painful steps toward the fence. "They are afraid that I might escape. Your worth is only that of a slave, but I am the pawn for the whole war debt. There is a guard here with me at all times." He glanced behind Jova, and a frightened look came to his face. The prince waved his hand as though to shoo Jova away and then quickly turned away from the fence.

Suddenly, a great pain stung Jova's shoulders, and a voice behind him shouted, "What are you doing here, dog? Get out of here! Do not bother the prisoner."

Jova turned just in time to dodge another swing of the guard's short whip. Quick as a greased pig, he ran toward the stream to fetch water for his master's household.

Chapter 3

The Whipping Cross

EACH DAY WHEN JOVA PASSED the stockade, he strained to see through the fence and catch a glimpse of Kaboo. Was the prince still there? Was he well? Did the Grebos feed him enough?

But always the guard seemed to be within sight, so Jova walked on without stopping and without seeing Kaboo.

Days stretched into weeks, and then one day there was a great commotion in the village. Word spread rapidly: The Kru king was coming to pay the war tax. All the village turned out, and Jova managed to escape his duties long enough to see the spectacle.

The rumor was correct. His king came leading a procession of several Kru men into the Grebo village. Wisely, they were not carrying any weapons that might infuriate their victorious enemies. And the

Grebos, not taking any chance that this was a trick, stationed their well-armed warriors along the pathway.

The Kru were burdened down with heavy baskets of rice and bundles of cassava roots and sugarcane. Behind them came a small herd of goats. They walked slowly, as though they were a funeral procession. On they came until the king stopped before the Grebo war chief. With a bowed head, the king said, "Here is the tax you demanded; now release my son." Slowly, the other Kru men set their loads of rice, cassava, and sugarcane before the Grebos and brought forward the goats.

With his head held high—in obvious contrast to the sad king's bowed head—the war chief looked down his nose and counted the riches set before him. "Where is the rest of it?" he demanded in a why-are-you-bothering-me voice.

The king's head snapped up, and his eyes flashed. Suddenly suspicious, he said, "What do you mean?"

"This is only half of your debt. Why have you taken so long to pay your debt when you bring me only half of what you owe?"

"You said the yearly tax was to be twenty baskets of rice, fifty cassava roots, ten bundles of sugarcane, and ten goats—and that is what I have brought at great hardship to me and my people."

The war chief sighed and rolled his eyes. "I demanded *forty* baskets of rice, *one hundred* cassava roots, *twenty* bundles of sugarcane, and *twenty* goats. Do not try to fool me."

The king's nostrils flared. His mouth became a straight, hard line, and he took several breaths before he got himself sufficiently under control to speak. "Must the Grebos add to their treachery with deceit? We did not wage all-out war on you, but you on us! In defeat, we have acted honorably in bringing this unjust war tax to you. My people have emptied their houses and have borrowed from their relatives in distant villages. We have nothing to eat and will have to search day and night for grubs and roots in order to survive until the crops you burned can be replanted and grow up to harvest. Why do you lie about the amount of the tax?"

Four Grebo warriors stepped forward with raised machetes, as if to attack the king, but the war chief halted them by raising his hand. Then he continued addressing the Kru leader. "As you can see, your head remains connected to your body only by my grace. We are the victors, so we can set the tax at whatever amount we please. See? Now I set it at *three* times what you have brought! What do you think of that?"

Before the stunned Kru villagers could react, he sneered, "Besides, it is good if you Kru must scrounge and scrape to stay alive. That way you will not have time to make war, and we will be safe from your revenge. What do I care whether you live or die? But if you live, I intend to make sure that you never regain your power, that you never rise again to threaten us. We intend to keep you as lowly as the chickens that scurry to move out of our path."

He turned to go back into his house when the Kru king cried out, "Wait! What about my son?"

The war chief paused but turned back only half-way. "Your what?"

"My son, the prince."

"Oh . . . oh, yes. You did leave a pawn with me, didn't you? I forgot. I don't know what's become of him, but one thing is certain: If you do not bring the remaining tax you owe, he will not have anything to eat." With that, he marched briskly into his house.

The king and the Kru delegation turned, and with bowed heads headed out of the village. But they had not taken more than a few steps before someone threw several rotten monkey plums at them. The plums splattered near the king's feet, and his men quickly gathered around him to shield him. The rotten fruit was soon followed by rocks and even handfuls of goat droppings as someone yelled, "Here's some Kru food. Eat that, you pigs!"—making a direct hit on the shoulder of the king's robe.

The king and his men pulled closer together and started to trot, trying to escape the village before they were injured.

Jova raced through the mob, too, attempting to keep up. He had to dodge between the people as they yelled and jeered. "Your Majesty!" Jova shouted. "I have seen Prince Kaboo. He is well."

The king kept running but looked over his shoulder and called back, "Watch out for him! Whatever you do, watch out for him."

Someone grabbed Jova by the arm and yanked

him to a stop. He looked up into the angry face of his master's second wife. She put out her foot and gave Jova a shove, tripping him to the ground. "Where do you think you are going?" she sneered. "Get back to the house!"

Two months went by, and Jova spent his eighth birthday with no celebration, no recognition. He worked just as hard and didn't get even an hour off.

From time to time, he managed to see Prince Kaboo briefly through the stockade fence as he went on errands. The prince remained brave, but Jova noticed that he was getting thinner. His cheeks were hollow, and his eyes peered from deep, dark sockets.

Jova began saving bits of his own food, wrapping them in leaves, and sneaking them to the prince whenever he could.

Then one day a delegation from the Kru village came bringing several baskets of rice, bundles of withered cassava roots, and a few thin goats. "This is all we have," said the man in charge as he placed the payment before the Grebo war chief. "There is no more rice, no more food in our village."

"I demand full payment!" roared the war chief as he pointed at the delegates. "Full payment must be made immediately. For each day that payment does not come, your prince will receive a public beating right here in our town square. That should inspire your lazy king to gather the taxes he owes. Now, get out of here and deliver that message to him!"

The delegation was driven out of town, and the next day at noon, Prince Kaboo was brought out of the stockade into the public square, where many people had gathered. There in the center were two logs protruding at an angle from the hard-packed ground. They were about five feet tall and crossed in the middle so that they made an X. Kaboo was brought to this cross and one hand was tied to the top of each log. His bare back was then beaten mercilessly with a whip made of poisonous vines.

Even before the beating ended, Jova could see great welts rising where the whip had struck. The poison in the vines was inflaming the skin even more than the strength of the blows. But Prince Kaboo did not cry out. He bravely suffered the whipping and was led back to the stockade, swinging his hobbled foot along in a shuffling stagger.

The next day the same thing happened, though this time there were welts on Kaboo's back even before the whipping.

That night as Jova was out feeding his master's goats, another Kru prisoner called to him quietly. "Did you hear what happened this afternoon?"

Jova shook his head.

"Wuledi escaped."

Jova's eyes widened. Wuledi was one of the Kru girls who had been taken captive. "How?"

"I'm not sure, but she was taken into the jungle with two other Kru girls to gather palm fronds. Just before they were to return, the Grebo who was in charge sent her off to get another armload. Then he brought the other two Kru girls back to town and left Wuledi out there. Everyone presumes she ran off through the forest for home."

Jova frowned. It did not sound like an escape; rather, it sounded as if she was *allowed* to run away. The next day after Prince Kaboo's whipping, Chiedi, another Kru slave, "escaped," though no one knew the details of how it happened.

After a week, there had been one escape per day, and Jova had an idea what was happening. The Grebo war chief was allowing one Kru at a time to escape to take a report back to the king concerning how his son was suffering. It was a cruel but powerful way to put pressure on their leader. The longer he delayed in paying the full tax, the more his son suffered.

Jova vowed that if the occasion arose, he would not go. He would stay and keep smuggling bits of food to his prince. Kaboo's health was failing rapidly. His back was a mass of open and infected sores. He was thinner and weaker than ever. The only good thing was that, in becoming so weak, he no longer seemed like an escape risk to the Grebos. They had at last removed the log-hobble from his foot.

Just before noon the next day, the Kru king and two assistants came to the Grebo village. This time, they brought only two baskets of rice, a bundle of immature sugarcane, and seven dead monkeys on a pole. But there was a fourth person with them, the king's only daughter, Mona, who was a couple years younger than Kaboo.

"You are a mighty warrior, one to be feared above all other Grebos," said the king as he knelt before the Grebo war chief. "We have brought you what we could."

The war chief looked over the offering with a sneer on his face. "You bring me monkeys when I demand goats? Who do you think I am? Only poor people eat monkeys."

"We *are* a poor people, O chief," said the king, lowering his head even farther. "We did not mean to insult you, but this is all we have. Have mercy on us and accept these articles in payment of our debt. Please, release my son."

"Bring him out," commanded the war chief.

Moments later, with one warrior on each side to support his arms, Prince Kaboo was dragged out. He was too weak to stand or even to hold his head up. When the warriors released him, he fell to the ground in a heap. In horror, the king started to go to him but was halted when Grebo spears touched his chest. He reached his hand out toward his son and pleaded, "May I take him home now?" Then, unable to control his agony at seeing his child's sad condition, the king began to weep.

"You may take him when you have paid your full debt!" snapped the war chief.

As tears streamed down his face, the Kru king said, "I have one further offer. Please allow my daughter to be pawn in place of my son. He cannot endure more. She, at least, is healthy and strong and could take his place for a while."

The Grebo war chief took a deep breath and looked from side to side at some of his advisers as he considered the offer, but before he could answer, there was a stirring from the crumpled body on the ground.

Prince Kaboo raised his head and in a faint voice said, "No. My sister must not take my place. Mona is younger and could not stand these beatings. Someday I am to be king. I am brave enough. I will endure the suffering."

Then he rose shakily to his hands and knees and began to crawl. The crowd which had gathered around parted to let him through, and then Jova saw where he was going. Prince Kaboo was heading toward the whipping cross! Slowly, step after step he advanced, his head hanging so low that his matted hair almost raked the dust.

When he reached the cross, he pulled himself up and flopped his broken and tortured body over the X, and there he waited.

Seeing his opportunity to put more pressure on the Kru king, the Grebo war chief nodded to one of his assistants, and the man quickly retrieved the whip. Everyone stepped back as he whirled it around his head and laid it with a resounding crack across Kaboo's ribboned back. Again and again the whip whistled through the air, finding its mark on the boy's deformed body.

It was the worst beating Jova had ever witnessed. A half hour later, the shaken Kru king was led weeping out of the town, and the people began to return to their activities. But Jova felt frozen to the spot. The little boy knew that Prince Kaboo could not take much more of this punishment. He would soon die.

Chapter 4

Escape Into the Jungle

TWO DAYS LATER, as Jova walked toward the stockade with a small ball of cassava mush for Prince Kaboo hidden in his hand, he noticed that the prison gate was wide open. He paused and approached cautiously. What was happening? Where was the guard? Jova couldn't see anyone.

He peeked in and warily entered the stockade. No one seemed to be present. Then, in the dark doorway of one of the huts, he spotted a small mound. After looking around to be sure no one was watching, Jova approached. It was a ragged, old blanket covered with stains and dirt. But when he got close, he could see that sticking out from under it, back into the dark interior of the hut, were two thin legs. One had the obvious wounds of the hobble log around the ankle.

"Kaboo? Prince Kaboo," Jova whispered. "Is that you? Are you all right?"

After a moment, he rallied the courage to step forward and pick up the edge of the dusty blanket. Kaboo lay staring up at him with an open mouth and wide, gaping eyes that did not seem to see anything. Jova jumped back in horror. His prince was dead!

But no, the staring, unblinking eyes moved just a little to follow Jova's movement. And then the mouth was moving, too, trying to say something.

Jova dropped to his knees and held his ear close as he strained to hear what his prince was saying. "What?" he urged. "Say it again."

"Water," came the faint whisper through a mouth so cracked and dry that it still hadn't closed.

Jova ran to find a drinking gourd, but it was dry. He grabbed it and raced out of the stockade and down to the stream. He pulled the plug and waited as the cool water gurgled in. "Faster, faster," he urged as he jerked the gourd back and forth under water.

When it was finally full, he raced back to the stockade. This time, he took no precautions to avoid being seen. Carefully, he dribbled some of the water into Kaboo's mouth. The first mouthful made the prince choke, and Jova worried that he had done something dangerous, but at last Kaboo managed to swallow.

For an hour or more, Jova stayed with his prince, feeding him tiny bits of cassava mush and getting him to drink more water. He found a rag and used some of the water to wash the sores on Kaboo's back.

Finally, when Kaboo could sit up, he noticed the open gate and whispered painfully, "Looks like . . . they're not worried . . . about me escaping . . . anymore . . . can't even crawl . . ."

When Jova had done all he could, he promised to bring food and water to Kaboo every day, and then he left. If he was going to serve his prince, he could not anger his master too much or there would be no freedom to sneak off to the stockade.

Apparently, the Grebos also realized that Prince Kaboo was near death, and they knew that a dead pawn wasn't worth anything. If the king's son was dead, the Kru people would have no incentive to try to gather more taxes.

So the Grebos decided that they would stage one last display. The next morning, they herded all the Kru prisoners to a clearing near the edge of the village. After allowing so many prisoners to escape to take word back to the king about how his son was suffering, only eight prisoners remained.

In the middle of the clearing, there was a large ant hill, and the prisoners were put to the task of digging a pit just a few feet from it. The digging was not hard, but the ants were disturbed, and frequently a few angry ones stung the diggers. When Jova took his turn, he was stung three times on his left foot. In a matter of minutes, his foot was swollen and burning with such fire that he had to be replaced by another digger.

When the pit was as deep as Jova was tall, the Grebo warriors who were guarding them told them to stop and listen to what the war chief had ordered.

"This pit is for your prince," one of the warriors began. "Tomorrow's beating will be delayed until sundown. If your king has not brought the full payment by then, his son will be buried in this pit with only his head sticking out. Then we will prop his mouth open with a stick and put honey on his face. First the stinging ants will do their work, and then the driver ants will come and eat his flesh, bite by little bite. Before the next morning, nothing but a white skull will be left here in this field."

Several of the slave prisoners began to wail, and the guards got angry. "Save your wailing," the head guard said. "There will be time enough for that if your king fails to rescue his son. Silence!" he shouted as he walked among them looking from one to the other.

"There is still one thing that *you* can do that might save your prince," he shouted—and this succeeded, as his yelling had not, to stop the loud wails. "Your prince needs a runner, the fastest one among you, to take this message back to his father. Who will it be?"

No one spoke. They were all staring at the ground.

"Come on now. Step forward. It means your freedom. And, if you are fast enough, maybe you can get the message to the king in time for him to gather the required rice and other items in time to save his son."

Still no one moved. All the slaves appeared to be busy counting their toes.

Suddenly, a rough hand hit the bottom of Jova's chin and jerked his face up to confront the angry warrior. "You!" he demanded. "Who is the fastest one here?"

Jova's eyes rolled from side to side as he tried to look around. His jaw was held so tightly in the warrior's grip that he could not turn his head. Finally, in a weak voice he replied, "She is." He pointed to Gami, a tall girl of about sixteen. Jova recalled the happy festivals the Kru people had enjoyed in former years. There had been games and races, and Gami had won every foot race.

"Then be off with you!" shouted the Grebo, raising his hand as though to strike the girl. "And tell your king the message."

All the next day, Jova listened for the arrival of the king, but he did not come. In the afternoon, Jova sneaked away from his job of splitting palm fronds for a new roof thatch on his master's house. He ran to the stockade to visit Kaboo, taking a little food and water. His gifts during the last couple of days had kept the prince alive, but Kaboo was still growing weaker and sicker. He could not even sit up.

"Why hasn't your father come?" asked Jova frantically. He knew it was a foolish question.

The prince was struggling to draw a breath. "Do not blame him," he wheezed. "He would . . . come if he had . . . anything to bring." He stopped again to catch his breath. "Our people are ruined . . . broken. They have nothing left to pay. . . . That is why my father cannot come."

Jova stayed with the prince as the afternoon passed, not caring whether he got in trouble or not. Then, when the sun was dropping below the trees that surrounded the village, two guards entered the stockade. They ignored Jova but picked up the weak prince by his arms, just under the shoulders. Again, the prince was so weak that his feet dragged on the ground; his head flopped down on his chest as though it were barely attached.

Jova followed them out to the whipping cross where they draped Kaboo's battered body across the logs without bothering to tie his hands. Soon a crowd began to gather. Everyone knew that this would be the last whipping, and for some ghastly reason, they gathered to watch.

When the war chief arrived, he looked around, saw Jova trying to hide behind some of the Grebos, and said, "Where are the other Kru slaves? I want all the prisoners here to witness this last punishment. I want all the Kru snakes to know how fierce we Grebos are. Never defy us, or this will be your fate.

Resisting our rule is useless."

The Kru prisoners, Jova along with the others, were pushed to the front to watch. A huge Grebo warrior stepped forward with a newly woven whip of poisonous vines. His muscles bulged, and an angry scowl contorted his face. He swung the whip around, making it whistle through the air.

And then, just as the whip was about to fall on Prince Kaboo's raw back, there was a blinding flash in the sky—brighter than the noonday sun—and a loud voice that said, "Rise up and flee! Rise up and flee!"

The man with the whip fell to the ground without having even touched the prince.

Everyone saw the flash and heard the words, but only Kaboo responded. His body peeled up off the whipping cross like bark being stripped from a tree. Slowly, he stood up straight and looked around. He took one tentative step, looking down as though he didn't know whether his feet would work or not. And then, to the utter amazement of everyone who watched, he ran at full speed across the open space toward the edge of the circle of those who had come to watch.

The crowd of Grebos parted as if they were water through which a swift canoe passed. Everyone stepped aside and allowed the prince to run through their midst unhindered. Kaboo dashed down the town's street and into the jungle.

For a few minutes, everyone stared with wide eyes, unable to believe what they had just witnessed.

46

Then total chaos broke out, and the crowd began to flow down the same street through which Kaboo had run. Jova ran with them, but when they got to the forest's edge, everyone held back. Within an hour it would be dark, and no one wanted to be in the jungle after dark. Not only were there wild animals to be concerned about, but the leopard men might appear and attack them.

In a few moments, however, the war chief began organizing his men, ordering them to collect torches and weapons to pursue the fugitive.

Suddenly, Jova realized no one was standing between him and the jungle trail. In fact, no one was watching him at all. Almost without thinking, he took off and ran down the same trail Kaboo had taken. Shouts and threats echoed behind him, but he kept running.

The mud of the trail felt cool beneath his feet. Vines caught his toes and nearly tripped him, but he carried on. Leaves slapped his face as the welcome gloom of the jungle closed around him. Far behind him came the sound of the Grebo warriors as they, too, set off down the jungle trail.

But somewhere up ahead of Jova was his prince.

Chapter 5

Lead, Kindly Light

J OVA RAN HARD. He had to catch up with Kaboo.
Kaboo was older and would know what to do.

Thorns stung Jova's legs, and he was getting winded from running so hard. But he and Kaboo were free! The last few slivers of afternoon sunshine pierced through the thick cover of leaves, turning the jungle into a shimmering Eden of greens and golds and browns and blacks with a bright ivory or lavender flower here and there.

If Jova could only catch Kaboo, all would be well.

But several minutes passed, and Jova had run

48

a mile or more, and still he saw no sign of Prince Kaboo. *How can such a weak person run so fast and so far?* he wondered.

The trail took a sharp turn, and then descended toward the river. With his heart pounding from exhaustion, Jova welcomed the easier, downhill path and let his legs stretch out to full stride. Then he tripped over a root, and before he could recover his balance, he went flying off the trail, through the foliage, and crashed headfirst into the trunk of a tall oil palm tree.

Everything went black.

How long Jova lay there, he never knew, but when he came to, the small patches of sky between the high branches of the trees were identifiable only by occasional stars. He sat up and was so dizzy that he lay back down and tried to think about his situation.

He could not hear any Grebo warriors, but he was alone in the jungle, and night had arrived. Back up the trail somewhere were the dreaded Grebos. Or maybe they had passed him while he was unconscious among the ferns. He did not know which way to go.

Even if Jova managed to avoid the searching warriors, he was far from home and alone in the jungle at night. There would be many poisonous snakes and rivers thick with crocodiles. He thought of elephants. They, too, could be dangerous, but they seldom bothered someone who was not bothering them, and they made a lot of noise. He could get out of their way in time.

But he could not escape the leopard. The big cats hunted at night and would attack if they were hungry and thought their prey was weak.

Worse still were the leopard men. No one seemed to know whether they were men possessed by the spirit of the leopard or leopards who took on the form of men. The few people who had survived an attack by the leopard men claimed that leopard men sometimes walked on two feet like men and sometimes on all fours like an animal. They spoke to one another like men but also screamed and snarled in the night like the great cats. They had spotted fur and terrible claws and ate human beings. But if they were men, that would make them cannibals! Jova shivered at the thought.

One thing was sure: No one walked safely in the jungle alone at night where the leopard men roamed.

Jova sat up again—more slowly this time—and this time his head did not spin. Slowly, he rose to his feet. There was a big knot on his head just above his left eye, but apparently nothing was broken, only sore and achey.

He took a couple steps in the direction he thought the trail lay, then looked around and tried to get his bearings. Far off between the trees, down near where Jova imagined the river ran, he saw a light. His first impulse was to run in the opposite direction, but it was not the flickering yellow flame of a torch that warriors might carry. Instead, a gentle white glow illuminated a small area as though a tiny bit of daylight was leaking into the dark forest.

Jova crept closer and peeked around a tree. What he saw amazed him even more.

In the strange, glowing light on the forest floor rested a large old log, and out of its hollow end crawled Prince Kaboo. Once Kaboo stood up and brushed himself off, the light began to move, and Kaboo followed. To Jova, his prince appeared completely healed of his wounds. He did not limp from the injuries of the hobble log, nor did he stagger as one who had been starved and beaten nearly to death. His steps were sure and easy.

With a start, Jova realized he was about to be left alone, so he moved forward. Once his feet assured him that he was on the path, he began to follow the light. Travel was not so easy for him as for Kaboo, however. The distant light gave him a direction, but it did not illuminate his way. Huge tree roots crisscrossed the forest floor above ground. Some extended out from the base of trees so high that they looked more like props than roots. Jova tripped and stumbled and crashed along, making so much noise that he was certain Kaboo would hear him following and run off in fear.

But Kaboo continued steadily along, sometimes stopping briefly to pick berries or fruit.

Keeping his distance, Jova continued to follow. When Jova came to the same places where Kaboo had found fruit, he felt around in the dark, also hoping to find something to eat. More often than not, he failed. But he did gather a few sweet morsels.

Through all this, Jova was uncertain what was happening. Was he dreaming? Had the knock on the head caused him to see strange visions? Or was this really happening?

In his mind, he reviewed what had occurred from the moment he first came to after his fall. It looked as though Kaboo had hidden in the hollow log to allow the Grebo warriors to pass by. Now that it was night, another strange light—though not so blinding as the one that had flashed at Kaboo's escape—was leading the prince through the jungle.

The scene was so astounding, Jova could not understand it. He considered calling out and making himself known to Kaboo and asking him what was happening. But he feared doing so in case the prince would run. Even worse, the whole scene might disappear, and he would find himself back on the jungle floor in the dark of the jungle night. So Jova kept silent, or as silent as he could as he stumbled along. In that fashion, he continued to follow the strange circle of light that dodged between the trees ahead.

Jova traveled that way all night, staying back just far enough that he would not lose sight of the prince or be seen himself.

As morning came, the light slowly faded—or, rather, it was swallowed up by the natural daylight that filtered through the trees into the jungle. As the jungle once again took on its familiar appearance, Jova became more convinced that he was not dreaming or seeing visions . . . at least not any longer. There was Prince Kaboo up ahead of him, walking

along through the jungle as if nothing unusual had happened. He disappeared behind one tree, only to appear a moment later from the other side. Everything seemed completely natural.

The only explanation Jova had for how he had gotten from knocking himself out with a fall the evening before to following the prince in the morning light was the mysterious event he had witnessed during the night. He had to accept it as true!

Working up his courage, Jova was about to call out or run ahead to catch Kaboo when he saw the prince turn off the trail. Kaboo pushed through the undergrowth until he stood between two fallen logs. There he lay down and pulled some large leaves over himself. He was hidden, just as he had been in the log the night before.

Jova crept closer. But at the distance of a stone's throw, he stopped. Something inside him prevented him from going closer. He decided to settle down and watch to see what would happen next. He found a large tree with high, exposed roots. Down between two of them, he crouched and made himself comfortable and completely hidden in every direction except facing Kaboo's hiding place. There he sat, intending to keep watch, but he was so tired that before long he fell asleep.

For the first time in months, his dreams were not filled with the frightening images of warfare and slavery among the Grebos. Instead, he dreamed of his home and the stream near his village where it went over a cliff and created a beautiful pool below.

When the sun shone through the forest leaves, the watery playground was filled with spray and the joy of children's laughter as they frolicked in the water. Jova was a good swimmer, but he had been afraid to jump off the cliff into the pool like the older boys. And then one day, Prince Kaboo had led him to the edge and urged him to take the leap. It was such a long way down, but his prince went first and yelled for him to follow. Finally, Jova had jumped down into the rainbow mists.

He awoke with a start, remembering his dream and the reality. Life in the village had been good. He had made that jump not once but hundreds of times after getting over his initial fear. On that day, he had begun to play with the big boys.

By now it was night again. Jova had slept the whole day away wedged between the winged roots of the tree. He stood up and began to crash through the undergrowth toward the trail, but in only a few moments he was hopelessly tangled in vines. He fought and pulled and struggled until, by the time he was free, he had completely lost all sense of direction. He was exhausted, and the panic that had grown almost familiar to him started bubbling up within him again. He tried to control it and keep it from driving him to run blindly into the dark. He must not do that. If he didn't crash headlong into a tree, he could get caught again in the bramble patch.

Finally, he calmed himself and looked around, trying to decide which way to go—when he saw the light again. This time, it seemed much farther away, almost out of sight. *Kaboo must have left before I awoke!* Jova thought. *I must hurry!* Now he had a direction, but keeping free of the vines slowed him down, and before he felt the familiar path beneath his feet, he had lost sight of the light.

Chapter 6

A Coward Turns Back

JOVA HURRIED AS FAST AS HE COULD through the gloom of the forest. But without the distant light to provide direction and help him see the silhouette of what was before him, the going was hard. Still he kept at it, sometimes stumbling or running into low-hanging limbs and vines, sometimes veering off the trail entirely and getting tangled in the undergrowth. After all, without the light, he had nothing but his bare feet to feel his way along the trail.

As far as productive travel was concerned, Jova found this method doomed. Once when he fell, his hand grasped a loose tree limb. He broke it at a

good length, stripped off the little branches, and used it for a walking stick. After that, the going was easier. He stumbled less and was able to feel ahead.

But he knew that for every two steps he managed, Prince Kaboo had probably taken ten with ease. He was falling hopelessly behind.

This discouraging thought had no sooner lodged in his mind when his foot splashed into water. Only his walking stick, which found a deeper bottom ahead, saved him from plunging headlong into some pool, or lake, or—what was it?

Jova stood perfectly still, alert for the sound of a crocodile slipping into the water to come and investigate what tantalizing meal might have graced his table. He heard a quiet gurgling sound several feet ahead of him and jumped back onto the muddy bank. But the gurgling did not seem to come closer.

What could move through the water but not come closer, or, for that matter, not seem to go anywhere? wondered Jova. His heart thumped so loudly it seemed to drown out the other night noises—the thousands of chirping frogs, the whir of bat wings in the trees overhead, even the gurgling in the water. He listened closely, and then the answer came to him with relief: It was not something going *through* the water that was making the sound but water going *around* something. He must be standing before a stream or river that flowed so slowly it was almost silent, except for a spot in front of him where a protruding rock or limb or root disturbed the water enough to make a gurgle.

A chuckle of relief escaped Jova's mouth, then broke into a laugh. As the tension and fear released, he roared so hard that he fell back onto the ground and held his stomach. As he did so, he happened to look up. There were stars in the moonless sky. They extended to the right and to the left, and, as he looked harder, he could see where the stars disappeared out ahead of him. No question about it. He was at the edge of a river that cut its way through the thick jungle—and a fairly large river at that.

But where was Prince Kaboo?

"Kaboo," Jova called hesitantly. "Prince Kaboo."

There was no response, so Jova called more loudly. Finally, he yelled, "Ka-boo-oo-oo," so long and loudly that it echoed through the forest.

Still no answer.

Jova worked his way along the bank, careful not to step on some sleeping crocodile, but the trail seemed to play out at the river's bank. He could not pick it up going right or left. This had to be a crossing. But what kind of a crossing? Could he wade across? Could he swim? He was a good swimmer, but . . . what about crocodiles? He wished there was a canoe pulled up on the bank.

In the dark he had no way of knowing.

Gradually he realized the truth. He had lost Prince Kaboo, and in the dark there was no way to find him.

Jova sat down and began to cry. This whole ordeal had become too much for the young boy. He couldn't continue. He couldn't endure one more trial, one more frightening event. It was just too much.

He cried and cried until he fell asleep there on the cool mud of the riverbank in an unknown jungle far from his home.

The chatter of monkeys and the squawk of birds woke Jova at dawn. They were upset about something, scolding and screaming. Something had invaded the privacy of their forest, and Jova didn't think they were complaining about him. He heard splashing across the river and peered through the morning mist. He saw the problem. The monkeys and birds were protesting the arrival of a half-dozen pygmy hippopotami, wading into the river along the far bank.

The fog swirled and hid them from his view. When it cleared briefly again, he could see that the river was shallow enough to be quickly waded and therefore probably safe from crocodiles, but the coming of the hippos was discouraging. With them munching tender water plants on the other side, he could not cross. An attack by angry hippos could be deadly.

He found some stones on the bank and threw them at the water pigs in an attempt to drive them off, but they did little more than flinch when a rock hit them. Jova yelled and shouted and waved his arms, but his noise disturbed them no more than the monkeys and birds had. The animals' eyesight was so poor that, as long as Jova kept his distance, they took no notice of him. And he wasn't about to get closer.

He waited, finding some grubs to eat under the bark of a rotting, fallen tree.

Finally, when the sun rose over the treetops and burned off the fog, the hippos headed upriver. Jova retrieved his walking stick and waded into the river. If any crocodiles approached, he might be able to scare them off by beating the water with the stick. At least in the daylight he could see them coming.

On the other side, the trail that had led to the river continued on, and, though Jova was not certain that Prince Kaboo had come this way, it was his best choice. Traveling during the day carried the risk of encountering some Grebos on the trail, but by now he was far from the village of the war chief, maybe even out of their part of the jungle. Still, he listened carefully as he went along.

When afternoon arrived, he began to think about catching up with Prince Kaboo. If the prince had traveled all night while Jova was stopped at the river, then pretty soon Jova might come to the place where the prince was hiding for his daytime sleep. But how would he know if he had caught up? What if he passed him by?

Again he began calling Kaboo's name, softly for fear of attracting some distant enemy, but loud enough so his prince could hear if he were holed up just off the trail. But as he walked along, there was no response. *What if he is sleeping soundly and can't hear me?* worried Jova. *Or maybe I passed him much earlier today without realizing it.*

When the forest started to darken with the coming of evening and he still hadn't found Kaboo, Jova gave up. He had not noticed any fork in the path, but his prince had either taken some other trail, or he had passed him while he slept in the woods. Tired and discouraged, Jova turned off the trail and walked a short distance through the jungle to where a small spring trickled cool water down a small cliff.

He drank his fill, then sat down to remove a thorn that had jabbed into his foot as he hurried along earlier that afternoon. He was in complete darkness before the small splinter came free. Then he leaned back against a fallen log to think.

His eyes closed in weariness, and for a few moments he floated free of his problems, dreaming of his home and the pleasant life of his village . . . before the Grebo attacks.

Suddenly, a sound startled him. It sounded like someone humming a song. He opened his eyes and blinked as he adjusted to the darkness. There, coming along the trail not more than thirty feet away, was Kaboo in his little circle of light! And Jova's ears hadn't fooled him. Prince Kaboo was humming a familiar childhood song as he swung along the trail. He didn't seem to have a care in the world.

Jova wanted to call out to him, stop him, join him. But somehow he couldn't. It was as though his voice couldn't make a sound, and yet he knew that he hadn't even tried. Why he didn't try, he didn't know. But he remained silent until Kaboo had passed him by and gone on down the trail, the mysterious pool of light dimly dodging among the trees as it had the first night.

Then, as though he had been released, Jova jumped to his feet and followed along.

The next morning when the dawn began to tease its gray light into the jungle gloom, Jova was watching carefully to see where Kaboo would hide. But instead of turning off the trail to look for refuge in a hollow stump or small cave, Kaboo stepped out of the jungle into an open field.

It was a huge field, larger than any garden Jova had ever seen in his village. And all across the field in orderly rows were small trees, no more than twigs with a few green leaves on them. They were newly planted coffee trees, though Jova had never seen a coffee plantation before.

From the jungle's edge, Jova watched Kaboo as he walked out into the middle of the field. When he headed toward the far corner, Jova followed, but not by walking into the open. He went around the field, keeping himself hidden at the edge of the jungle. He had to move fast in order to get to the other side and see where his prince was going.

Kaboo took a wide path leading from the corner of the field through more jungle. Jova also took this path, staying well back out of Kaboo's sight.

They traveled in this way for about an hour as the road went up one hill and down the next. Always, Jova was ready to duck into the jungle should Kaboo look back. Why he was afraid to be seen, he didn't know. He wished he had contacted Kaboo the first night. Now he felt foolish to have followed so long without revealing himself. So he hung back.

Then, as Jova came to the crest of the final hill, he looked down into a large plain where no jungle grew. There were other roads and houses, and out on the plain stood a huge city, a city of white houses with red roofs. Jova had never seen such a place! But even more amazing, he could see white people walking along the roads and outside the city.

He had heard stories among his tribe about a white man named Doctor Livingston who came through the jungle and traveled on toward the mountains where no Kru or Grebo had ever gone. He talked about a God of love and looked at funny marks in a black book. It was said that he had invited some of the village men to go with him, but none would dare go. That was long ago, when Jova's father was young.

Now Jova could see many white people and black people, too, like himself, walking around the buildings of the city. But the sight of white people scared Jova. Then he noticed that Kaboo was walking down the road into the city. How could he do that? What was he doing?!

Frightened, Jova watched for a long time.

He had heard that white people were devils. Some

said they were spirits, but either way, Jova wanted
nothing to do with them! He almost ran after Kaboo
to beg him not to go into such danger, but his courage failed him. It was as if roots had grown from his
feet into the ground. All he could do was watch from
the hilltop as his prince drew closer to the white
buildings.

Sunshine bathed the top of the low hill where
Jova kept his watch, but a great, gray
cloud hung low over the white city

and seemed to touch the ground just beyond it. Jova remained at the edge of the jungle all day, hoping Kaboo would return. Sometimes the cloud dropped down onto the city and swallowed the houses. Then, a few hours later, it would rise and release them.

When the sun rose the next morning, Jova finally gave up waiting for Kaboo to return. He couldn't stay here; he had to go home. With a sinking heart, he turned back into the jungle. He knew he had been traveling west while following Kaboo, so he headed east. Fear of the big cats and leopard men was his constant companion as he wandered through the jungle. Weak with hunger, on the third day he finally came to a village of Kru people. They were not part of his king's realm, but at least they were not Grebo and did not return him to the Grebos for a reward. He stayed in the village for several weeks until a trading party set out toward his village, and he traveled with them.

When he arrived home, everyone was amazed to see him. His family had given him up for dead! The village had already heard from other escapees about the flash of light and the voice that had freed Kaboo. But why hadn't Kaboo come home? Had their prince been saved from the Grebos just to fall prey to wild animals in the jungle?

Jova was afraid. No one would believe his story of Kaboo following a light through the jungle. But if they *did* believe it and discovered that he had turned back from following his prince out of fear, they would call him a coward.

As the villagers bombarded him with questions, Jova cautiously told about escaping the same day as Prince Kaboo and his adventures in the jungle: tripping and hitting his head on the tree, coming to the river in the dark, having to wait for the hippos to go up river, and finally coming to the friendly village. But he never said a word about following Kaboo to the white city.

For six long years, Jova had kept his secret. But now his tribe needed a new king, and he was the only one who knew where their prince had gone.

Chapter 7

Journey to the White City

Many things had changed in the six years since Jova had followed Prince Kaboo to the white city. He was now fourteen, the same age Kaboo had been when he had walked courageously down into the city. Would Jova be brave enough to do the same on a quest to find his prince?

Jova had graduated from the bush-devil school. He had the tattoo scar on his forehead to prove it. But had it given him courage? He knew much more about the jungle than he had when he had wandered alone in it six years ago. But the jungle was still a dangerous place to travel by oneself.

Nevertheless, this was a quest that he must make alone. Even if he wanted a companion, he doubted whether anyone would believe his story now that it had been held in silence for so long. And even if someone did, that person would mock him for turning back as a coward.

On the other hand, if he brought Prince Kaboo home to give his people a new king, all would be forgiven and forgotten concerning why he had turned back the first time. No, it was clear. He had to go by himself. No matter what the danger, he would find his prince. It was the opportunity of a lifetime. In finding Prince Kaboo, Jova could save his people, earn a king's fortune, and prove himself to be a great warrior.

All that day as he gathered the things he would need for his journey, Jova thought about his trip through the jungle six years before. In the bush-devil school he had learned about many new plants that could be eaten, how to make a small snare to catch monkeys, what roots made a medicine that would take away the sting of a scorpion. The bush devil claimed powerful magic. But Jova had never seen him do anything as powerful as the flash of light and the voice that had freed Prince Kaboo. The bush devil had never healed anyone so near death as Kaboo had been.

Most important, the bush devil was a cruel god who seldom did anything good for people and never did anything without demanding a high payment. For six years, Jova had thought about Kaboo's release. It must have been the work of some great god, far more powerful than the bush devil.

This god must be very different than the bush devil, too, Jova decided. He had not demanded any payment, and he had acted with unusual love and care in providing the light that had guided Prince Kaboo. Jova had tripped a thousand times over roots and stones as he had trailed along in the dark. But the light had shown Kaboo every step. Jova had not seen him stumble even once. *It must be a very loving god to care for Kaboo like a father,* thought Jova. The bush devil was certainly not loving, nor were any of the other spirits the Kru people worshiped. Usually they just put curses on people.

That night before Jova went to sleep, he prayed quietly, "Oh, great god of the light, guide me as you did Prince Kaboo so that I may bring back to my people a king who will save them." Then, with an easy feeling in his heart, he went to sleep.

The next morning, Jova simply told his mother that he was leaving to become a warrior. She cried but knew she could not stop him. Her tears made him feel bad. She probably thought he was going off to fight Grebos or hunt leopards, and she feared for his life. Not wanting her to worry, he whispered, "Be easy, Mother, I'm going to find Prince Kaboo. Everything will be fine."

But she cried all the harder. "You go on a fool's errand, my son. After six years, he will not be found."

Jova wanted to tell her that he knew where Kaboo had gone and that the god of the light would be with him, but that would bring up a story much too long for their brief goodbyes, even if she could believe it. So he hugged her and said nothing.

After a week of traveling through the jungle using his new survival skills, Jova found the white city. He was encouraged to find it was much as he had remembered. There were hundreds of houses, many with white walls and red-tile roofs. He could see white people going and coming. His memory had not played tricks on him, except for one thing— beyond the city was a huge lake. Water stretched all the way to the afternoon sun, and the shores to the north and south did not even begin to curve to form the ends of the lake.

Could this be the everlasting sea that was mentioned in Kru legends? A great flood must have brought it to the white city since Jova had first seen it. Then he remembered the gray cloud that had hung over the city the first time he saw it. Today there was no cloud. Maybe the sea had driven it away. A question came to Jova's mind: *Is it better to be swallowed by the sea or by a cloud?* He decided that the sea was more dangerous. After all, the gray cloud had been over the city six years ago and the city had still survived. But today the sea threatened; it was very close to the city. He had better find Kaboo soon.

Not having ever seen the sea before, Jova did not

realize that the reason he hadn't seen the sea on his first visit was because it was hidden behind a fogbank that drifted in and out over the shoreline. Today, there was no fog, and the sea sparkled clearly beneath the hot sun.

He took a great breath to gather his courage, then marched down the road toward the city. This time he did not turn back but forced himself to continue until he had entered the very streets of the city.

The sights he saw amazed and frightened him. A white man rode on a great beast, larger than a cow, though not as big as an elephant. Strange music and the smell of exotic foods teased his senses. By the white man's calendar, it was the beginning of August, 1892, but this was something Jova was not to learn for some time.

The very day Jova arrived in the city, he set about asking all the people he passed if they had seen Prince Kaboo. It was then that he discovered how many languages humans spoke. Kruan was quite common, and he was able to communicate with many of the black people. But there were others: Mandingo, Kpwesi, Gora, and Bulom. And, of course, there was the white man's language—maybe more than one. Jova couldn't make any sense of its strange sounds.

All afternoon he walked the streets asking anyone who would listen about Kaboo, but people just shrugged or shook their heads.

While traveling through the jungle, Jova had

been able to gather berries, pick bananas, or find grubs for food. He even caught some fish in a stream. But in the white city, all the food belonged to other people. It was not like his village where food from each family's hearth was shared with whoever was present at mealtime.

As evening approached, Jova hung around the marketplace until he saw a woman loading her fruits and vegetables into baskets. Two crying children clung to her legs and hindered her work. "Can I help you?" offered Jova. "I will carry your baskets wherever you wish if you will give me one of those yams."

The woman agreed. After carrying the baskets to the woman's hut on the beach, Jova eyed the waves rolling up onto the sand with suspicion. To him, they looked like a snarling cat practicing its pounce on an unsuspecting prey. But the sea seemed to be staying in its bed, so, after he finished helping the woman, he went off to build a small fire and roast his yam. Later, he fell asleep on the sand under an upturned canoe.

He awoke at dawn with the waves lapping at his feet. Not understanding the natural rise and fall of the ocean's tides, Jova jumped up in fear, certain that the sea was rising to flood the white city. At the same time, he noticed that the cloud had returned and covered the sea, the beach, and the city so that he could not see farther than he could throw a stone.

"This is a terrible day," he said to himself. "The white city is doomed, and I have not yet found Prince Kaboo." He hurried off to the marketplace—where he had found the most people the day before—and began again to inquire about Kaboo.

He was so busy with his quest that he did not notice until afternoon that the cloud had disappeared and the sun shone brightly in a blue sky. That evening, having earned some scraps of food by doing odd jobs for the same woman, he returned to the beach to see how much farther the sea had come in its attack on the white city. To his great surprise, the water had retreated. This puzzled him so much that he ran back to the market woman's hut and asked her who had driven the sea back. She laughed at him, explaining the tides. "There is no reason to fear the sea except during great storms," she said. "Even then, it does not invade the city."

This Jova found hard to believe. He promised himself that he would watch the sea carefully from then on to see if it really did go back to its bed twice a day like the woman said.

By the third day, Jova was discouraged. Maybe he wouldn't find Prince Kaboo after all! But in the marketplace he saw an old man sitting in a booth that he had not seen before. The man was carving ivory into beautiful haircombs, knife handles, and amulets. Jova watched in admiration for a few minutes as the man worked.

Then, remembering his purpose, Jova said, "I'm looking for Prince Kaboo. Can you tell me where he is?"

The man worked silently for a few moments as though he hadn't heard Jova, but then he glanced up and responded in a familiar accent, "Prince, you say.

Why do you seek this Kaboo?"

"He is to be king," Jova blurted, unthinkingly, "and I must find him and bring him back to our village. Do you know him?"

The man frowned at his work as he made one final gouge to complete the small ivory turtle he was carving. He held it up to admire. "I have heard of a Kaboo," he said slowly. "He is Kru, isn't he?" The man turned to look at Jova. There was a sly grin on his face, and three parallel tribal marks scarred his right cheek.

The old man was a Grebo!

A chill went through Jova. He clapped his hand over his mouth and turned to flee. Even over the noise of the busy marketplace, Jova heard the cackling of the old man's laugh behind him.

What have I done? thought Jova as he darted between booths and carts pulled by bullocks. *Now the Grebos know I'm looking for Kaboo!* But the man had said, "I have heard of him." What did that mean? Had he heard about Kaboo's captivity under the Grebo war chief? Or had he heard of his presence in the white city?

Jova redoubled his efforts. But after that scare, he was much more careful who he asked. He checked the person's right cheek and asked some other questions first to see if the person spoke with a Grebo accent.

Watching for tribal marks paid off, too. One day Jova saw a boy not much older than himself rolling huge barrels along a dock by the sea. And this young man had a Kru tribal mark between his eyebrows, much like his own.

"I'm looking for a Kru named Kaboo," Jova said after making sure the dock worker spoke his language. "Have you heard of him?"

"Kaboo? Why, yes, I knew him." The dock worker grunted as he rolled a heavy barrel. "We worked together on a coffee plantation north of town, but he's not there now. Last I heard, he lives with white missionaries and paints houses."

Jova could hardly contain his excitement. He listened carefully as the dock worker told him where to find the white missionaries in a far part of town. No wonder he hadn't found Kaboo! Jova had spent all his time looking around the marketplace and along the beach. He had thought those were the logical places to search since that was where the most people gathered each day.

It took a lot of questions to find his way to the mission, which was almost like a small village within the white city. There was a bamboo fence circling several houses inside, which faced a central yard of hard-packed dirt. Jova hesitated. Did he dare go inside? Finally, he saw three black men come out of one of the houses, so he found courage to step into the yard.

"Can you tell me where the white missionary is?" he asked them, trying not to let his voice shake.

The men shrugged. There were several at the mission, they said, but they led him to one of the houses.

Jova didn't know how he was going to make a white person understand him. He certainly couldn't speak their language. But when a white woman came to the door and was told by the black men that he wanted to speak to her, she welcomed him in the Kruan language.

Surprised and relieved, Jova spoke boldly. "I am looking for Kaboo. He is a boy from my tribe." He had decided not to say "prince" or speak of the need for a king until he was certain such details wouldn't be carried to Grebo ears.

"Oh, I'm sorry," said the white woman. "Samuel's not here—we call him Samuel Morris now. He changed his name when he became a Christian."

"Became a Christian?" said Jova, not knowing what that meant.

"Oh yes, he had a most dramatic conversion. He was wonderfully changed. I would love to tell you all about it."

Jova was taken aback in confusion. How was Kaboo changed? What did it mean? Had he become white? Jova looked around to see if the Africans who had brought him to the missionary woman's house showed any signs of becoming white. By that time, they were walking away. But they looked just the same as the people in small villages—except for the strange clothes they wore.

Finally, he found his voice again. "But where did he go?"

"He took a ship to New York nearly two years ago."

"A ship?"

"Yes. You know, a big boat that goes to sea," said the woman, realizing that the boy from the jungle who stood before her had no idea what a ship was. "New York is far across the sea. It takes a long time to get there."

"Oh," said Jova. His shoulders sagged in despair. Had he come this far only to be stopped by the sea?

He shook his head to clear his thoughts. He was thinking like a child. He must think like a man! After all, he had found someone who not only knew who Kaboo was but knew where he had gone! And if Kaboo had traveled on the sea, why not he?

Jova straightened his shoulders and stood tall. "Well, where do I find this ship-boat?"

Chapter 8

Across the Great Sea

THE MISSIONARY WOMAN STOOD with open mouth and raised eyebrows, amazed at Jova's question. Finally, she managed, "I'm sure I do not know where that ship is . . . but Samuel wouldn't still be on it. He went to New York."

"Yes, I understand that," said Jova. "But I want to go, too."

"Well, it's . . . it's not that easy." She studied Jova for a moment. "Young man, do you have a place to stay? I mean, you don't live here in Monrovia, do you?"

Monrovia! So that was the name of this big village. "No,

I don't live in the white city. I was sent by my king."
Jova looked around to make sure there were no
Africans listening—Africans who might be Grebos.
"Our king is dying," he continued in a quiet voice,
"and Kaboo is our prince. I must find him and bring
him back to our people."

The woman nodded. "Well, you would be welcome
to stay here while you look for a boat to New York.
We have work you can do, and you can learn English."

Stay with the white devils? Jova quickly shook
his head and started to withdraw, but the woman
said quickly, "You'll need to learn some English to
find a place on any ship to America."

Jova paused. What the white woman said made
sense. He knew when he had set out that finding his
prince—proving that he was a brave warrior—would
take courage. So once again Jova swallowed his fear,
agreeing to work at the mission in exchange for
English lessons.

The missionary's name was Miss Knoll, and she
said he could learn English by attending her daily
Bible classes. One day, Miss Knoll's Bible lesson told
about a man named Saul to whom God spoke with a
loud voice from heaven and a blinding flash of light.

"That's what happened to Prince Kaboo!" said
Jova, proud to be able to contribute to the class
discussion.

"So he told us," said Miss Knoll with great curios-
ity. "But how do you know?"

"Oh," said Jova with a big smile, "I was there. I
saw it."

This report excited Miss Knoll greatly, and she had Jova go over every detail. As Jova warmed to the story, he even found himself telling about the trip through the jungle where the strange light led Kaboo. By this time, he had grown to trust the other Africans in the class and did not fear that they would laugh at him.

As he talked, Miss Knoll got a faraway look in her eyes, and when he finished, she didn't quiz him about why he had lost courage to follow Kaboo down into the city. Instead, she began to hum a song and then quietly added the words in English,

> *Lead, kindly Light, amid th' encircling gloom,*
> *Lead Thou me on;*
> *The night is dark, and I am far from home;*
> *Lead Thou me on:*
> *Keep Thou my feet;*
> *I do not ask to see the distant scene—*
> *One step enough for me.*

After a few moments of silence, Jova ventured, "What was that song, Miss Knoll? I did not understand more than a few words."

She smiled shyly, her eyes still glistening with unshed tears. She bit her lip and sighed. "It's a hymn—one that meant a great deal to me when I was in Taylor University. I felt God calling me to follow Him, but I was scared. That hymn helped me follow and obey Him one step at a time. And," she threw her hands up into the air with a tilt of her head, "He brought me here."

She stood up and translated the words for her students. "Maybe together we could come up with a Kruan version of the song. Would you like that?"

Not far from where the mission station was located, it was possible to see any ships that anchored near Monrovia to unload and load their cargoes. Most ships were too large to enter Mesurado Lagoon, which was crowded with smaller boats. But, when the weather was calm, larger sailing vessels often lay at anchor offshore for a week or more as longboats and other small craft serviced them.

Whenever a new ship arrived, Jova raced down to the docks to meet the crew, looking for the captain. Whenever he spotted the captain or another well-dressed officer, he ran to the man and said some of the English words he had carefully learned. "Welcome to Monrovia, Captain. You take me to New York, yes? I work plenty hard."

For weeks, he was ignored or, at best, received a scornful laugh, but then one day there were two ships at anchor, one a sleek new schooner and the other a weathered old trader. As soon as Jova identified the crew of the schooner, he approached them. "Are you going to America?" he asked.

"Straight away," answered an officer in a blue uniform.

"You take me to New York, yes? I work plenty

hard for you."

The man glanced at him with a sneer. "Passage is one hundred dollars, not a penny less," he barked and walked off.

Discouraged, Jova turned away, but just then he caught sight of the gray-haired captain from the old trading ship. His longboat had just tied up at the dock, so Jova approached him with his question.

"What did you say?" responded the captain as he stretched some of the kinks out of his bones. He had an inquisitive frown on his face and was looking right at Jova.

"I say, welcome to Monrovia, Captain. You take me to New York? I work plenty hard."

The captain stroked his beard slowly as he eyed Jova. "The last time I stopped here a young African said the same thing to me. But he was a little older than you. Tell me, why do you want to go to New York?"

Jova was so excited that anyone had bothered to pay him any attention that he blurted out in a loud voice, "I must find Prince Kaboo. He went to New York."

The captain shook his head and started to move on past several Africans who were working on the dock. One of them was watching Jova closely. "Sorry, lad," said the captain. "I never heard of any 'Prince Kaboo.' Besides, you're a little young to be going to sea."

In desperation, Jova touched the captain's arm to beg a moment more of his time. "Samuel Morris," he

blurted. "You know Samuel Morris?"

"Sammy?" said the captain, a broad smile cracking his leathery, old face. "Of course I know Sammy. He changed my life and the life of nearly every man on board my ship. What about him?"

"I go to New York to find Samuel Morris. He is Prince Kaboo."

With his faltering English, Jova finally made his wishes known and discovered that it was on this captain's ship that Kaboo had traveled nearly two years before. The old captain was eager to tell his story, and Jova had such a hard time understanding his fast-spoken English that he finally persuaded the captain to spend the evening at the mission station where he could have help translating.

Around the dinner table, with the aid of Miss Knolls and one of the African pastors, the captain told this story:

When Sammy first asked me to take him to New York—just like young Jova, here—I cursed his brashness and said I would never take someone like him on board.

But he calmly said, "Oh yes, you will. My Father said you would."

"Where's your father?" I asked.

"In heaven," was his answer.

I walked away, disgusted, but the next morning when we brought our longboat ashore, he repeated his request. "Get out of here," I said with a kick to his pants. But that evening when we returned, there he was waiting by the boat. When he made his request for the third time, I finally said, "Well, what can you do?"

"Anything," he said.

So, thinking that he was an able-bodied seaman, I took him on. But once we had lifted anchor and were at sea, I found that he knew nothing. I was angrier than a cat with a knot in its tail, and I took it out on him every day, making him do the dirtiest work. I was a harsh master and angry that I had been fool enough to take on this landlubber. One night I was so drunk when Sammy reported to me, that I slugged him with my fist and knocked him out. But when he came to, he carried on with his work as if nothing had happened. At the time, it made me all the more angry.

Then, during a storm, one of my men fell from the rigging and injured himself severely. He couldn't even rise, but Sammy knelt down and prayed for him. The man immediately got up and carried on as though nothing had happened to him . . . except after that the sailor had the utmost appreciation for Sammy.

This got my attention and everyone else's, too. Sammy was always asking me and the men if we knew Jesus. When we would curse and swear at him for such a question, he would kneel down and pray for us. In time, it got me to thinking about God and the Gospel as I remembered it from my childhood.

Before we got completely away from the African coast, a severe storm damaged the ship beyond seaworthiness. We were lucky to put in behind a small island where, for two weeks, we made repairs. Though Sammy was young and small, he kept at the pumps like my biggest men, all the time claiming that the Holy Spirit gave him the strength.

When repairs were finally completed and we were again under sail, I made the mistake of giving out extra rum to let the men celebrate. Unfortunately, it led to a brawl, mainly led by a big man from Malay who wanted to kill all the whites on board—a regular mutineer. Thinking he had the support of some of his Asian friends and could overpower the rest of us, he grabbed a cutlass and charged us, ready to kill.

Then Sammy stepped in his way and simply said, "Don't kill."

The blade was held high above Sammy's head, and I knew that the Malay hated blacks even more than whites. He had specifically sworn to kill Sammy when I first brought him on board. And to tell the truth, I had expected him to do it long before this because he had killed many other Africans in the past.

But for no reason that any of us could see, the Malay slowly lowered his weapon and went below deck. Every man who saw this happen was impressed. Sammy represented a power stronger than our meanest sailor.

I went to my cabin with Sammy, and he immediately began praying for the men. Before I knew what I was doing, I was praying, too, and confessing my own sins.

That was how I found Jesus as my own

Savior. That same day, I vowed never to reward the crew again with rum.

By the next morning, the murderous Malay was dreadfully ill. He was as sick as I've ever seen a man, and I didn't expect him to live out the day. But Sammy was not discouraged. He went to visit and pray for him even though this was the man who hated him and had vowed to kill him. And God answered Sammy's prayer, too. The man recovered immediately and thereafter treated Sammy like a brother.

Sammy started holding church services on deck, and every man participated—not grudgingly, but eagerly. Sammy's faith transformed the whole spirit of my ship, and I'll be forever grateful.

"So," concluded the captain, "if you are a friend of Sammy's, you are a friend of mine. And if you want to go to New York, I'd be more than happy to take you. In fact, I'll pay you for what work you do during the passage. It'll make a man of you."

Jova could hardly believe his ears. Even the missionaries and the African pastors laughed with delight over Jova's good fortune. As the captain put on his hat and stepped to the door, he said, "Be at the dock at dawn tomorrow, Jova, and we'll have a place for you."

Jova was so excited he could hardly sleep that night. When he arrived at the waterfront early the next morning, the sleek schooner had already sailed, but a longboat was waiting to carry him out to the old trading ship.

Chapter 9

Assassins

FIVE MONTHS LATER—in April of 1893—with a little money in the pockets of his whiteman's clothes and amazement in his eyes, Jova looked down at the crowded docks along the East River of New York. The captain came alongside and put his hand on Jova's shoulder.

"New York's a big place," he said sympathetically. "But when Sammy left us, he went to Stephen Merritt's gospel mission on Eighth Avenue. We heard some great reports of how he preached to the people at the mission. I don't know if he's still there, but if I were you, that's where I'd start looking. I'll send one of the crew to show you the way."

The captain summoned the ship's carpenter, a friendly New York native who seemed only too glad to leave the unloading to the other crew members. Jova turned and waved goodbye to the captain as he and the carpenter walked down the gangplank.

No sooner had Jova's feet hit the dock than he felt dizzy and had to grab the carpenter's arm to keep from falling. "What's the matter, son?" laughed the old sailor. "You still got your sea legs under you?"

The strange sensation of being on firm ground again passed in a few moments. As they headed up Pike Street away from the docks, Jova saw two black men standing in the shadows of a warehouse door. They turned away when Jova looked at them . . . but not before he saw what looked like three dark scars on their right cheeks.

A wave of terror clutched Jova's chest, as though someone had just hit him in the stomach. Grebos *here?!* What were Grebo warriors doing here in America? Why had they come all the way across the sea?

"Did you see those men?" Jova asked his companion anxiously.

The old carpenter frowned and looked back over his shoulder in the direction Jova had indicated. "You mean the ones back there at the warehouse?"

"Yes. Two black men."

"I saw them," shrugged the carpenter. "What of it? Just a couple dock hands lookin' for a job."

"Did you see them watching me?" asked Jova. "When I look at them, they quickly turn faces away, like trying to hide."

"Hey, what's eatin' you? Probably just talkin' to each other."

"You not see anything strange about them—their faces, I mean?"

Instead of answering, the carpenter turned up his hands in a gesture of helplessness and kept on walking.

But as they worked their way through the streets of New York, Jova couldn't get the experience out of his mind. Jova had let slip the purpose of his search to the Grebo ivory carver in the marketplace in Monrovia. But even if the Grebos wanted to stop him from bringing Prince Kaboo back to the village, how could they have known he was coming to New York? If they had seen him leave Monrovia, how could they have known where he was going? Or how could they have arrived first?

It all seemed too impossible. There couldn't be anything to it. *It must have been the shadows or a smear of dirt on their cheeks,* he told himself. All the same, he looked behind him one more time to see if anyone was following. There was a carriage a block back and some children chasing a hoop, but otherwise the street was empty.

He sighed with relief and hurried on. Soon, they were passing through Chinatown; then came a part of town where the white people were all talking a language other than English. It was like visiting many different countries all within walking distance of one another. Jova couldn't believe how big the buildings were, and he had never imagined that so many people existed in the whole world.

The streets were full of carriages pulled by horses.

He smiled at how surprised he had been when he first saw a man riding a horse in Monrovia. But then he saw a big carriage going down the middle of the street without any horses or oxen pulling it.

"Where are the horses?" he asked the carpenter.

"That's one of the new horseless carriages," the sailor grinned. "It runs on gasoline and doesn't need any horses. And look at the lights on those poles. They use electricity to shine at night. No one has to go around and light them every night. They just pull a switch at Mr. Edison's light company."

Jova shook his head. He could hardly believe all the new things he was seeing. But he couldn't let himself get distracted. The important thing was finding Prince Kaboo.

When they arrived at Stephen Merritt's gospel mission, the graying Bible teacher welcomed Jova warmly. He was a short, wide man, a little round around the middle, with a big, friendly smile. But Jova waited until the ship's carpenter left to tell him about trying to find Samuel Morris.

"Oh, we certainly remember Sammy," said Stephen Merritt. "Why, that lad brought a great revival to our mission! The first night he gave his testimony, seventeen men gave their hearts to Jesus. The same kind of thing happened in every church he visited around here, too."

"But . . . you mean he isn't here?"

"Oh no. He went out to Taylor University in Indiana to study the Bible. But I'm so excited that you've come all the way from your country to learn about Jesus, too. This is amazing!"

Jova didn't know what to say to the man. He had not come to study the Bible. He had come to America to find Prince Kaboo and bring him home. The Bible study he had attended in Monrovia had been interesting, and Miss Knolls had urged him to give his life to Jesus, but Jova had not understood. Besides, he had another purpose in life. He was on a quest for his prince, and he wasn't going to let anything stop him.

Jova sighed. He was tired from all his travels. He wished he could go back home. "How do I get to this Taylor University?" he said wearily. Would he ever catch up with Prince Kaboo?

"Indiana? Hmm, you're a bit young to go to the university," mused Mr. Merritt, rubbing his chin thoughtfully. "But you seem like a determined young man. The best way to get there is by train. Guess you don't have any trains in your part of Africa—at least, Sammy had never seen one. But a train is a big machine for traveling. . . ." He paused, searching for words.

"Is it a horseless carriage?" asked Jova.

"Why yes. It is something like a horseless carriage. How do you know about those? Do you have automobiles in Africa already?"

"Oh no. But I saw one of yours today, and I would love to ride in it to Taylor University."

"Well, a train is a little different. It has several cars hooked together."

"But it doesn't use any horses, does it?" Jova was excited at the idea of riding on a machine without horses.

Mr. Merritt smiled. "You've got the right idea, but a train is much larger and goes much faster than an automobile. It has a steam engine that pulls it from the front. But it also costs a good deal of money to travel on it."

"I have money," said Jova proudly, pulling out the handful of coins the captain had given him after his voyage.

"That's a nice start," said Mr. Merritt, "but I don't think it will get you to Indiana. However . . ." again he rubbed his chin and studied Jova, "for a young man so interested in Christian education that he would come all the way from Africa, there *may* be another solution."

Jova tried hard to follow the English words, but he wasn't sure exactly what Mr. Merritt was saying. "When Samuel was here," the man went on, "we organized the Samuel Morris Missionary Society to raise money to send him to Taylor University in Indiana. There's still a little more money in that fund." He beamed at Jova with his big smile. "I'm the treasurer and would be glad to use some of that money to help you, too."

The next morning, Stephen Merritt wasted no time in withdrawing some money from the bank. Before Jova really understood what was happening, he was standing in a New York train station with a ticket to Fort Wayne, Indiana.

Jova rode the train all that day, spending much of his time looking out the window at the passing countryside that was bursting with spring flowers and new leaves. Just before dark, he sat up quickly as the ground beside the train dropped away. Then he realized that the train was traveling on a bridge over a large river, but the bridge was so narrow that the train seemed to be flying through the air. When he looked down from the window, all he could see was the water below. What a marvel train travel was! It took his breath away.

After eating some bread and cheese Mr. Merritt had given him in a small bag, he shut his eyes and tried to sleep. But with all the excitement of coming to America and riding this marvelous, strange machine, sleep wouldn't come. After a while he decided to stretch his legs by walking through the cars. Going from one car to the next in the blowing, cold night air was frightening, but he had seen others make it safely. Gripping the handholds tightly, he stepped from one swaying platform to the creaking, groaning platform of the next car. He practically fell against the door and pushed it open. This car was a sleeper and had curtains pulled over each berth with only a narrow aisle to pass through. But the next car forward was a coach like his own.

He walked all the way to the front of the passenger section. "Can't go any farther," said a train man in a dark suit and a little pill cap with a gold band around it. "That up there is the mail car." So Jova returned to his own car. But just as he sat down, he noticed two black men sitting in the last seat at the back. His heart lurched, and he ducked down. Could they be Grebos?

No, that was crazy. There were thousands and thousands of black people in America. Two of them on the train in his car didn't mean anything. But his heart was still pounding. He turned his head to sneak a peek, but the lamps in the coach car had been turned too low for him to get a clear look.

He began to think through his whole quest again. If they were Grebos, how had they known he was coming to America? Then he remembered the afternoon on the dock in Monrovia when he had met the captain of the ship that had brought him over. He had been so excited that he had told him all about Prince Kaboo. Could he have been speaking so loudly that others overheard him?

He squeezed his eyes shut and tried to recall the scene. There had been other Africans working nearby on the dock. Could they have been Grebos? *Oh no. Oh no!* thought Jova as a sweat broke out all over him. *That was it. They heard me, and now they are*

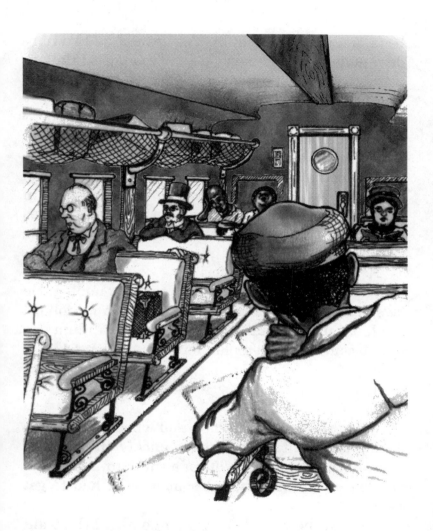

following me. They've followed me all the way here!
His mind was working fast, and he recalled the
speedy clipper ship that had also been anchored
offshore that day. The clipper ship's captain had said
that it, too, was going to America, only the price had

been one hundred dollars. That would be two hundred dollars for two men—a lot of money—if the two at the back of the train were Grebos. But maybe it was not too much to pay if they were being sent by their tribe. There were many Grebos who worked for wages in Monrovia.

Jova sneaked another look toward the back of the train. The men were sleeping, but one of them had turned in his seat so that his face was more fully in the light. Jova froze. There were three dark stripes on his cheek. This was no smear of dirt or trick of the shadows.

He was a Grebo warrior!

Jova sat back in his seat, his heart pounding. He *was* being followed. And the only reason for following him must be that they intended to kill him. He had to come up with a plan for escape—fast.

When the train screeched and wheezed to a stop during the night, Jova slipped quickly off the train and ran through the streets of a small town. He had no idea where he was, but somehow he had to get away.

Finally, the whistle blew and he heard the train chug out of town. He breathed deeply of the frosty air and relaxed. His plan was in motion. Slowly he headed back toward the train station. He would catch the next train to Indiana while his enemies traveled on ahead of him. Somewhere down the line they would realize he was gone, but, in this strange land, they would have no idea where he was.

But when he came around the corner of the station, his plan turned into a nightmare. The two Grebo men stood in the moonlight right before him.

Jova froze. An evil grin crossed the face of the shorter warrior. Jova tensed for a blow, sure that they would strike him immediately. But instead, they each stepped aside, bowed, and with their arms motioned Jova to walk between them.

I'm dead, thought Jova as he looked from one to the other. *Together they are planning on killing me, probably by hitting me right in the back.*

Nevertheless, he mustered all his courage. He had known from the beginning that he might lose his life on this quest. He would not turn back in fear as he had done when he was a young boy on the hill overlooking the white city. He stepped forward and walked between them, expecting a knife blade to strike him any moment.

But it did not.

He walked between his enemies without receiving so much as a scratch. As they walked along the deserted station with one warrior on each side, Jova had to resist the overwhelming urge to run. When they came to the door of the train station, the two Grebos ushered him in. Jova sat down on a bench in the dim light and suddenly realized he was alone.

The Grebos had not come into the station with him.

Slowly, an even more frightening thought crossed

Jova's mind. *If they did not kill me when they had the perfect chance, then they must have some other objective.* His mind raced for an explanation, but when it came, it was no comfort. *They must be following me to get to Prince Kaboo!*

It was the only explanation. They didn't care about him. They wanted to remove the future Kru king.

They were assassins!

Chapter 10

A Desperate Leap

JOVA SAT ALONE IN THE TRAIN STATION, knowing that somewhere outside lurked his deadly enemies, the enemies of his people. A large clock on the wall ticked away the minutes that stretched into hours.

For the first time, Jova recalled how the men had looked. One had been tall and thin with a nearly bald head leaving only a rim of hair above his ears and around to the back. He was clean-shaven, with a square jaw and deep-set eyes. His face had seemed chiseled out of ebony—expressionless and cold. But even in the moonlight, Jova had seen the traces of the three scars on his right cheek.

The shorter man had been more muscular, with a round face and a trace of beard. He had been wearing a round-topped hat—a bowler hat, Jova thought it was called. As he thought about this man, Jova remembered that when he had grinned, a couple front teeth were missing. *They were on the opposite side from the cheek scars. So it was his left front teeth that were missing,* Jova thought.

But what difference did it make? He had been told that in America, just like in Monrovia, there were police to protect people from criminals. Maybe he could go to the police, but . . . who would believe his story? "Two assassins have followed me all the way from Africa to find and kill my prince. You must arrest them." Anyone would laugh at such a complaint. So far, the men hadn't committed a crime. They couldn't be arrested solely on the basis of Jova's wild fears.

The clock in the train station ticked on, and Jova got up and walked from window to window. He wiped the fog off the cold panes and looked out to see if the men were lurking outside. There were two gas street lamps burning on either end of the platform beside the train tracks, but Jova couldn't detect anyone in the shadows. It was no comfort. He knew they were still there.

He returned to the bench and lay down. In time, he fell into a fitful sleep. When he awoke, he looked up at the clock. He was glad that he had learned to tell time while living at the mission station in Monrovia. It was 4:25 in the morning. It would be getting light before long, and an eastbound train would soon arrive. Jova could give up and go home. Or he could wait for the next westbound train and continue on to find Prince Kaboo.

If he continued on, he would lead the assassins to his prince—and in so doing, bring death to him. On the other hand, if Jova gave up his quest and headed home, that might draw the Grebos off Kaboo's trail . . . but that was no answer. If he gave up, the Grebos would still win. Kaboo would not return home to reclaim his throne, and his people would be weak and without a leader.

Every way Jova looked at his dilemma, those seemed like his only options. But there had to be another way. He went over each detail again in his mind: His enemies wanted to prevent Kaboo from claiming his throne. Clearly, the Grebos would believe assassinating him was the most certain way to do that; that's why they were following Jova. But the Grebos would also succeed if they kept Jova from finding Kaboo, if they scared him into returning back to Africa without contacting the prince.

Slowly, a new plan took shape in Jova's mind.

He did not wait for the next westbound train. Instead, when morning's first light met the eastbound train as it groaned and screeched and puffed to a stop outside the small train station, Jova walked dejectedly toward it as though he had given up in defeat and was returning to Africa. He got on the last car, paid the conductor some of the money he had earned on the ship, and found a seat near the window where he could watch the station platform. Just as he expected, moments before the train left, his two pursuers jumped on the car ahead.

They were still following him.

Then Jova remembered something: last night just before it had gotten dark, the train had crossed a trestle spanning a river. How long had that been before he had gotten off in the small town to escape the Grebos? Had it been an hour? Two hours? He couldn't be sure; so much had happened. But the train had crossed a large river on a bridge that was so narrow the train had seemed to be flying across.

If Jova could time it right so that he jumped from the train just as it traveled over the bridge, he could drop into the river, swim to the bank, and escape without the Grebos knowing that he had gotten off the train.

He hoped to trick the Grebos into thinking he was still on the train. It was similar to the plan he had made when he got off the westbound train in the small town the night before. But last night, he had been going west. Now he was going east. If the Grebos continued on, they would not know where he was.

His plan had failed the night before because they had been watching at every stop. When they saw him get off, they, too, got off. But if he leaped from the train while it was speeding down the tracks, no one would think to be watching for him.

Jumping from a fast-moving train onto the hard ground would certainly result in injury, if not death. But Jova was a good swimmer, and he had often dived from the cliffs into the pool at the bottom of the waterfall near his village. If he could time his jump from the train to land in the river, it might result in a neat escape. The best part of the plan was that no one would know that he had left the train, especially not the Grebo warriors.

Twice, as he looked out the window at the lay of the land ahead, it seemed as though they might be approaching some kind of a river. The flat land was replaced by gentle, rolling hills that slowly lost elevation. New spring grass was coming up everywhere, and baby buds put a green mist on all the trees.

The first time it looked as if they might be coming to a river, Jova got up quickly from his seat and walked to the back of the car and opened the door. He stepped out onto the small platform. The crisp morning air buffeted him as he leaned around the back of the train car to watch ahead.

Unfortunately, they were crossing only a small creek.

The second time, Jova didn't even go out into the cold. He soon saw that it was only a small stream they would be crossing.

But then as he looked out the right windows at

the prairie stretching off to the south, broken only by groves of just greening trees, he saw a ribbon of silver snaking off to the south in the brilliant morning sunshine. It was a river. They were coming up on a river.

On the platform at the back of the last train car, Jova made himself ready. He unhooked the small safety chain on the side of the platform and took three steps backward. There was just enough space for him to get a good jump. He peeked around the left side of the train. It was navigating a gentle curve that led onto the trestle. The smokey, churning engine was just venturing out onto the spindly bridge.

I hope it is strong enough to hold the train, thought Jova. Then he reminded himself that he had already ridden a train that had come safely over the trestle from the other direction. Besides, he had more important things to think about. In spite of how narrow the trestle looked, he would have to jump far enough out to miss the timbers that supported the bridge. He tried taking a practice run across the platform. There wasn't much distance to get up his speed.

In addition to clearing the trestle, he would also have to time his jump just right to land in the water below. He could now see that the river was quite wide, but the train was carrying him forward. He would not land directly below the point where he jumped. As he fell the twenty feet or so into the river, he would continue moving in the same direction the train was going. Therefore, he would have to jump before he came to the place where he wanted to land.

But this was it. There was no time to practice.
He was almost there. The sound of the wheels

under him changed as his car—the last car on the train—rolled out onto the trestle. He could see the river. He was almost over the edge of it.

He braced himself.

Then, just as he was ready to go, the back door of the train coach opened and a white woman in a big bonnet stood there with a look of horror on her face. He had to go *now*, before someone stopped him! Jova gave her only a momentary glance before he took three powerful steps right past the surprised woman. She screamed as his foot left the platform, and she kept on screaming as he fell toward the water—and his possible death.

His heart sank. He had not made a clean get-away. She had seen him and had announced his departure to everyone in the train car. Whether he survived or not, he had failed in his purpose of escaping secretly.

Splash!

He hit the water much harder than he had imagined he would—much harder than when he used to land in the pool below the cliffs near his village in Africa. The impact knocked the breath out of him. Dark green water closed over his head, wrapping him in the grip of its icy fingers. *Cold, so cold!* This was not a tropical stream or the waves on a sunny African beach. This was a swift river in North America where the snow and ice of winter had melted only a few weeks before.

Chapter 11

Riding the Rails With Hoboes

WHEN JOVA FINALLY fought his way to the surface of the river, he was gasping and struggling with the swift current that seemed determined to pull him under again.

He fought hard, driving with powerful strokes for the shore. Then his foot hit something, and he recognized it as a submerged log. The log extended from the deep part of the swift river to the shore. There the stump and a large tangle of roots rose above the surface of the water and tucked itself tightly into the muddy bank.

Jova pulled himself along the length of the log until he could grasp the roots and secure some relief from the powerful tug of the current. He rested there, hanging on to the roots with his body still in the water. Taking in great gulps of air, he was conscious that he had come much closer to losing his life than he had expected.

As he regained his breath, the chill of the water began to have its effect, and he shivered uncontrollably. He had never been in water so cold that it actually hurt, making his arms and legs ache to the bone. Jova started to crawl out of the river when suddenly he heard the mournful whoop of the train whistle, followed by a metallic screeching sound. Cautiously, Jova looked up over the edge of the riverbank. The train had come to a stop a half mile or so down the track. He stood up to his knees in the icy river, his head just over the rim of the bank, as he watched a most disheartening event begin to unfold.

The train engine belched a great billow of black smoke. White steam boiled from its wheels. And then . . . it began to back up ever so slowly. Jova frantically looked around for a better place to hide. On the west side of the river was a forest with plenty of cover, but on the east bank where he had found refuge, it was open prairie. The only tree was the huge fallen log behind which he hid. And the only way he could remain hidden was behind the root mass, which meant continuing to crouch in the icy river.

With more groaning and hissing and clanking, the slowly backing train stopped just before it rolled out onto the trestle that stood on its spindly legs above the river. Jova could hear the engine sighing and grumbling like some enormous, living beast. Mr. Merritt had called it an "iron horse," but it sounded more like an angry, wounded bull elephant to Jova.

Passengers lined the windows on the side of the train that faced Jova. Some had lowered their windows and were leaning out, pointing toward the river. The train cars were close enough that Jova could have thrown a rock and hit one, but he pressed himself against the muddy roots of the fallen log. After a few minutes of confusion, the train conductor and several other men climbed down out of the last car and walked out on the trestle over the middle of the river. A woman—obviously the one who had opened the door just as Jova jumped—stood on the car's platform and yelled directions to the men on the trestle.

"No. Go a little farther . . . a little farther . . . there! He jumped right about there."

"Are you sure, ma'am?"

"Of course I'm sure," she yelled. "I opened the door just as he jumped."

Jova ducked even lower. Two figures had climbed up on top of the last train car and were standing there, shielding their eyes with their hands as they looked down into the water. They were black men— one short and one tall.

"I don't see anyone," yelled the train conductor.

By this time, another train official was standing on the platform beside the woman. He yelled back to the man on the trestle. "If she's right and someone did jump, there's no way he could survive a fall like that."

"Well, I *am* right," snapped the woman indignantly, making sure her voice was loud enough for those out on the trestle to hear. "I saw him with my own eyes!"

"Of course, madam," patiently replied the conductor on the trestle. "But unfortunately, the river has gotten him. It's fast, and it's cold."

"He's dead for sure," said another man out on the trestle.

"Shouldn't we search for the body at least?" demanded the woman.

"Why waste time? You said he was a black boy, didn't you?" said the conductor on the platform.

The woman turned to look at him indignantly. "What's that supposed to mean? What an awful thing to say!"

The conductor shrugged. "Let's get going. We've got a schedule to keep!" he called to the men on the trestle. Then he turned to the woman next to him. "Don't worry about it, ma'am. We'll report it at the next stop. All aboard," he bellowed.

Jova saw the two black men on the roof of the train turn to each other, then climb down to join the other passengers as they crowded back onto the train.

Soon the whistle blew, and a jolt clanged from car to car as the engine wheezed and puffed and spun its great driver wheels, straining to set the train in motion again. Within a few minutes, the train was out of sight with only a wisp of black smoke drifting away on the wind.

Stiff and aching, Jova climbed out of the water. The river had been so cold that the chilly April air blowing through his wet clothes felt warm by contrast. But it didn't ease his shivering. With his teeth chattering, he climbed back up to the train track and made his way over the trestle, then headed west at a jog. It was half an hour before he could slow down to a walk without starting to shiver again.

But a change of mood had come over him. Instead of fearing that he had failed when the woman noticed him jumping from the train, Jova found himself feeling hopeful. Everyone on the train—including his enemies—seemed to think he was dead. He could continue his quest. It didn't bother him that he was nearly out of money in this strange land and still far from Taylor University. In fact, he had no idea how much farther he had to travel to get to the university, but, one way or another, he was going to find Prince Kaboo.

Late that afternoon, Jova saw a collection of buildings in the distance and gratefully realized that he was approaching a town. The people there could tell him how to get to Taylor University. It wouldn't be long now.

But before he reached the town, he saw several people camping in a little grove of trees beside the train tracks. One man waved him over, inviting him to join him at his small fire.

"Name's Jack," the man said, motioning Jova to sit down on an upturned crate. He plopped some beans on a tin plate and held it out. Jova gratefully took the plate, scooping the beans into his mouth with his fingers just as the man did. The stranger's clothes were so dirty that they all seemed the same color. In fact, the dirt had buried itself so deeply into the pores of his skin that his face was nearly the same shade as his soiled clothes.

"Been ridin' the rails long?" the man asked with the rise of one of his bushy eyebrows.

" 'Riding rails'? I don't know riding rails."

"You know, travelin'. Have you been travelin' long?"

"Oh yes," said Jova. "Many, many months I come . . . riding rails."

"Hey. You talk funny. You're not a regular farm-hand, are ya? Where ya from?"

"Africa," said Jova brightly as he licked his lips with the last bite of beans. "I come . . . riding rails . . . from Africa, through jungle and across the sea and behind the iron horse. I'm on a quest."

"Ya don't say. Ridin' the rails across the sea, huh?" grinned Jack as he began to chuckle. "Hey, Daniel," he yelled toward one of the small shacks tucked under a nearby tree. "Get yourself over here and meet a real African."

"A what?" came back the voice of an unseen person.

"A *real* African. He even talks different than you."

"What do you mean? I *am* a real African."

"Not like this, you ain't," chuckled Jack.

Jova jumped with surprise as an old black man in a rolled-brim hat came out from behind the hut and walked toward them on bowed legs.

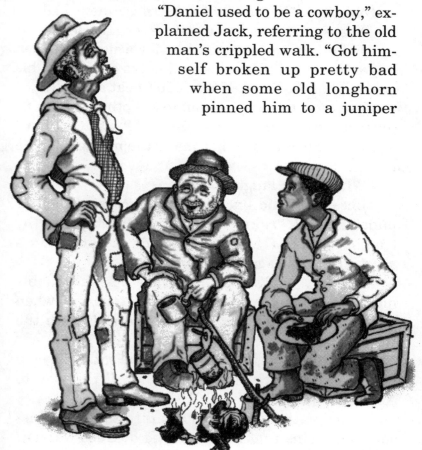

"Daniel used to be a cowboy," explained Jack, referring to the old man's crippled walk. "Got himself broken up pretty bad when some old longhorn pinned him to a juniper tree out in California."

To Jova's relief, Daniel did not have three scars on his right cheek. Ever since he'd seen the Grebos near the dock in New York, he had checked out every black person very carefully. But this was the first American black person he had met face-to-face.

Daniel rubbed the white stubble growing out of his dark chin and eyed the young traveler sitting on the old crate. "You really from Africa?" he asked.

"Yes, sir. I come riding rails across the sea."

Daniel stared openmouthed for a moment, then broke into a great laugh, holding his sides with his gnarled hands. "Well, if that don't beat all."

Jova looked from one man to the other not knowing what they found to be so funny. "It was very hard work," he offered, but that made them laugh all the harder.

"Why do you laugh at me?"

"Because," said Jack when he got his laughter under control, "ridin' the rails means travelin' by train. That's what us hoboes do. I don't think there's any train tracks across the ocean."

"No, sir," said Jova, and then he realized his mistake and laughed, too. "No. I go on the ship when it comes across the sea but ride the rails with the train."

"Now you got it," said Daniel as he sat down on a wooden box. "But what brings you all the way to America? Where ya headin'?"

Realizing that he had to ask directions of someone, and seeing that Daniel wasn't a Grebo warrior,

Jova told his story.

When he was finished, Jack said, "Where'd you say this prince of yours was?"

"At Taylor University," said Jova. "Mr. Merritt bought me a ticket, but I got off the train."

"I never heard of Taylor University. Have you?" said Jack, turning to Daniel.

"Nope." The black cowboy pulled a corncob pipe out of his shirt pocket and knocked a few ashes out of it, dug around in the bottom of the bowl, then put it in his mouth. He reached for a twig and held it in the fire to light the pipe with.

Jack pointed a gnarled, dirty finger toward Jova. "You still got the stub of that ticket?" he said.

Jova dug in the pocket of his pants and pulled out the soggy remains of an orange ticket.

Jack shook his head. "That's sure not gonna do you much good now. Leastwise, you couldn't get back on any train with it."

"Do ya even know what town you were headin' toward? Where is this Taylor University?" asked Daniel.

"Yes, sir. Fort Wayne, Indiana," said Jova. That's where Mr. Merritt had told him to go.

"Oh, well, that ain't so hard then," said Daniel, grinning around his pipe. "We can put you on the midnight freight, and you'll be there by noon tomorrow."

Jova enjoyed the rest of the evening with his two new friends and met some of the other hoboes in the camp. Around each campfire, he was offered some small morsel of food—a slice of dried bread, a cup of squirrel stew, a few spoonfuls of creamed corn from a can. As midnight approached, Daniel and Jack walked with him up to the train tracks. Lacy clouds drifted across the moon and painted the landscape in ever-changing patterns of silver and charcoal.

"Now, you see that water tower?" said Daniel, pointing to a huge, dark tank on stilts that stood beside the train track. "When the train stops to take on water, you just run up and climb into one of the open boxcars. Make yourself to home, and you'll be there by noon."

Jova looked up and down the tracks, two lines of shiny cold steel that divided the countryside for as far as one could see. "You mean I don't have to pay? I had to pay when I got on the train before."

"That's 'cause it was a passenger train. This here's a freight. If the car is empty, it's because they're takin' it somewhere to fill it up. Might as well hitch a ride when you can."

"But how will I know when I'm at the right stop?" asked Jova, still concerned about the details of the plan.

Daniel looked at Jack and shrugged. "Well, what do ya say, Jack? How *is* he supposed to know when he's reached Fort Wayne if he ain't never been there before?"

"Ask someone."

"There you go," said Daniel, patting Jova on the shoulder. "You just gotta ask someone."

That idea seemed a little shaky to Jova. "What if

no one is around?"

The two hoboes looked at each other. "He's got a point," muttered Jack. "It wouldn't do to ask a train-man. Could get his head cracked that way."

"What do you mean?" asked Jova.

Jack held up his hands as though he were sur-rendering to the law. "Look, son. Ain't no harm in ridin' in empty boxcars. They gotta move 'em from one point to another anyway. Don't take nothin' away from nobody. It's not like it was stealin' or nothin'. . . but some train officials don't approve. So we stay clear of 'em best we can, and then there's no trouble."

"Oh, come on, Jack. Why don't you just go with the kid? Keep him company. You could use a change of scene."

"Me? You been in this here hobo camp longer than me. Why don't you go with him?"

Daniel considered. "Why don't we both go?"

"It's a deal." The two men shook hands and slapped Jova on the back.

When the freight arrived and stood idly on the tracks taking on water, Jova's new friends found an empty car with a pile of straw at one end and pulled him on board. When they were settled warmly into the straw, Daniel dug in his pockets and came up with two slightly bruised apples. "Here, rations for the road." He took a bite and passed one to Jova.

The train jerked. It was no sooner rolling at full speed than Jova fell fast asleep.

Chapter 12

Prince Kaboo

DANIEL'S TATTERED BOOT nudged Jova's leg. "Wake up, man."

Bright sunshine silhouetted the old cowboy standing in the open door of the boxcar. He swayed slightly back and forth in time with the clickety-clack of the train wheels. "Time to wake up. We're almost there."

Just then the mournful train whistle sounded from the engine.

"This is Fort Wayne?" asked Jova as he rubbed his eyes and brushed the straw from his hair.

"Be there in about ten minutes. You been sleepin' 'round the clock. Now, you best be gettin' up 'cause we're gonna jump off before this train stops in the train yard."

Jack, who had been standing in the shadows, added, "That way we won't attract the attention of any trainmen."

"I already jumped from a moving train once," said Jova, shaking his head, "and it was no easy thing."

"Don't worry," said Jack. "We'll be goin' slow enough that even old Daniel with his bum legs can make it."

As they stood in the open door of the boxcar watching the countryside race past, Daniel turned to him and said, "Couldn't help noticin' that scar ya have in your forehead running up from your nose. Musta been a pretty nasty injury. What happened?—if ya don't mind me askin'."

Jova touched his fingers to the scar. "Oh, that was no accident. It's a tribal tattoo. It shows I'm from the Kru people. Prince Kaboo will have one, too. But if you see any men with three marks on their right cheek, stay away from them. They are Grebo warriors and not nice."

"Hmm. I knew a feller who had three scars on his left cheek," mused Daniel. "He wasn't very nice neither—'course word was that he got those three scars from a mean old bear he tangled with one night."

The train slowed to enter the town. When it was not going much faster than a person could walk, they dropped to the ground and hurried down the bank into a thicket.

"Now," said Jack once the train had passed, "if you head right along this trail, it will come to a road. Turn left, and you'll be in Fort Wayne in no time."

"Where are you going?" asked Jova.

"Oh, there's a hobo camp back this other way. We'll find some friends there. You'd be welcome to stay with us if you don't find your university."

Jova smiled. "Thank you very much. But I must find Taylor University. I must find Prince Kaboo."

Waving goodbye to his friends, Jova eagerly hiked along the road until he came to the small city of Fort Wayne. Could he really be so close to finding Prince Kaboo? He had never seen a university before, so when he passed a large wooden building on West Main Street, he went to the door and stepped inside. Inside, his eyes widened. He'd never seen such a strange sight.

The building was like a huge barn with a wooden floor, and on the floor several gaily dressed young people were gliding past on strange shoes with small wheels under them. They all seemed to be going around and around in a large oval, accompanied by music being pumped out by a man sitting at a large wooden box in the corner. He was using his hands and feet to make the music change notes.

"Is this Taylor University?" Jova asked a man who was sweeping the floor.

"The university?" laughed the man. "Does this look like a classroom to you?"

"I don't know," said Jova. "I am from Africa, but I

am looking for Taylor University."

"Africa? Say, you wouldn't be Sammy Morris, would you?" said the man as he leaned on his broom, eyeing Jova. "No, of course not. You couldn't be. You're too young and much too dirty. Besides he *goes* to Taylor University, so he would know where it is."

"You know him?" said Jova eagerly.

"No. But one night there was a revival service right here in this roller-skating rink, and he was here. People came from all over the county just to be prayed for by him, so I hear. But I didn't come. I had to take care of my sick grandma. Maybe I should have brought her here. There was plenty of talk about him the next day. Some people claimed people got healed when he prayed—"

Eager to be on with his quest now that he was so close to his goal, Jova broke in. "Excuse me, but could you just tell me how to get to the university?"

"Oh, sure," said the talkative janitor. "But you're lucky you got here in time. They're going to move the university to Upland pretty soon. In fact, I heard that for the ground breaking, the railroads are fixin' to send special excursion trains down to Upland. Now, ain't that a kicker, going *down* to *Upland. Down* to *up*—get it?"

Getting more and more impatient with the man's chatter, Jova again broke in, "But where is the university now?"

"Well, if you keep going down this street . . ."

Once Jova had the basic idea of where to go, he excused himself and left before the man got started with another of his stories.

But as he was going out the door, the janitor called after him, "I'd advise you to clean up before you go to a university. You don't look presentable enough to be meeting educated people."

Jova took the man's advice and brushed himself off as well as he could, washing his face and hands in the St. Mary's River, which flowed through the town. When he came to some large buildings, he kept asking questions until he found the main office of the university. The white woman behind the desk smiled and told him that Samuel Morris was indeed a student there.

"However," said the woman briskly, "he's not on campus right now. He has taken ill and is in the hospital."

The woman must have seen the boy's shoulders sag. Her voice softened, and she called to another student and asked if he would show Jova to St. Joseph Hospital.

Jova was trembling as he walked down the long hall to Kaboo's room. He had come so far . . . could he really have found Prince Kaboo after all this time?

He knocked on the door and heard a soft voice respond in English, "Come in."

There, lying on the white pillow, was the ebony face of an African about twenty years old. He had well-balanced features with strong cheek bones, bright eyes, and a square jaw. His eyes were clear, but he looked thin, and as he rolled his head to see who his guest was, Jova could see that he was weak.

And then Jova had a shock. There was no Kru tattoo on the young man's forehead!

As he stood there uncertainly, the figure in the hospital bed looked at him closely, and then his eyes widened in surprise. "Jova?" the young man said, a great smile splitting his dark face. "How did you get here? I am so glad to see you!"

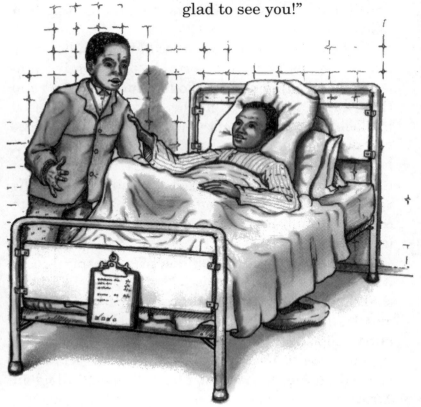

"Prince Kaboo!" Jova cried. "It is you! But . . . but, you do not have a Kru tattoo on your forehead. I thought . . ." Jova was so overcome with joy and relief that he couldn't continue.

Kaboo smiled weakly. "Do you forget that I was taken by the Grebos as pawn before I went through the bush-devil school, so I never received my tribal mark. But . . . that is a long time ago. How did you get here? Why have you come?"

Jova finally found his voice. "I have come to get you," he said huskily. He had found his prince at last.

With tears, the two embraced and soon began to fire questions back and forth in their native language. Jova explained all about following Kaboo and the strange light through the jungle. He confessed his lack of courage in not going down into the white city the first time. "But I am older and braver now," he said, lifting his chin. "And our tribe is in great need of you. I am sorry to bring you sad news, but the king, your father, is dying. Our people need you to come back and be their king so we will not appear weak to the Grebos."

Kaboo looked out the window of his hospital room with a far-off look in his eyes. "I want to go back," he said finally, "but I have been talking to my Father, and He has not promised me that I will return. I must keep speaking to Him."

Jova was puzzled. "What do you mean? How can you talk to your father? Isn't he still in our village in Africa?"

"If he is still alive, yes. But I was speaking about my heavenly Father, God in heaven. I talk to Him all the time. He helps me in all things. . . . Except," he said after a bewildered pause, "I do not understand why He has not made me well. Last winter when my ears froze—oh, it gets so cold here. You would not believe it, Jova!—but when my ears froze they hurt very much, and when I prayed, my Father made the hurting quit right away. But now I can't seem to get well. I don't understand it."

"You'll be well, soon," Jova said confidently. "And then we'll go back to Africa where it is warm and pleasant."

The reunion was interrupted by another visitor, a pleasant-faced middle-aged white man whom Kaboo introduced to Jova as Professor Stemen. "One of my favorite teachers," Kaboo smiled.

After hearing the amazing story of Jova's quest to find his missing prince, the professor immediately invited Jova to stay at his house, which was right across the street from the hospital. When Jova finally left Prince Kaboo's hospital room to get a much-needed meal at the professor's house, Professor Stemen said to Jova, "I'm glad you have come. We are worried about Sammy. He's just not getting well like he should."

Jova looked up from his bowl of hot soup at the professor's grave face. "What do you mean?"

The professor leaned both arms on the table, worry lines etched in his handsome face. "The doctors think Sammy has dropsy. They say he could be facing heart or kidney failure—probably stemming from the cruelty he suffered years ago when he was a captive. They . . . they fear he may not live."

Chapter 13

Taking Home a King

WHEN JOVA CAME TO VISIT KABOO the next day, the prince was smiling. "Last night," he said, "I talked to my Father, and now I understand why I am not getting better, and I am happy."

"Good," said Jova, remembering that talking to his Father meant that Kaboo had been praying to God. He was becoming more and more impressed with this praying.

The evening before, as Jova had sat at the dinner table, Professor Stemen told him about how Kaboo's faith had virtually saved the university. Just a few months earlier, the university was on the verge of closing. Its money had run out, and the board of trustees had decided to close its doors. They could no longer afford the cost of their buildings in Fort Wayne. "But Sammy," said the professor—Jova still found it hard to think of Kaboo as Sammy—"felt we should pray. And so we did. Then at the next meeting of the board, one of the members suggested that if we couldn't afford to remain in Fort Wayne, we ought to move the school to Upland, Indiana. That seemed impossible, but he said that he would look for a cheaper location and financial support. Within just one day, enough money had been raised to purchase new land and move the school. It was remarkable!"

Jova heard similar stories from other people about how God had answered Kaboo's prayers. So he was eager to hear what Kaboo had heard from "his Father" about his sickness.

Kaboo pulled himself up in his bed until he was in a sitting position with pillows stuffed behind his back. "I am so happy," he said. "I have seen the angels. They are coming for me soon. The light my Father in heaven sent to save me when I was hanging helpless on that cross in Africa was for a purpose. I was saved for a purpose. Now I have fulfilled that purpose. My work here is done."

"That is good!" said Jova. "So now we can go back to Africa?"

Kaboo shook his head, and a slight sadness briefly dimmed his smile. "No. I will not see Africa again. My work here on earth is finished."

Jova stared at him blankly as the meaning of Kaboo's words slowly sank in. Could it be that his prince was going to die? No! Not at a time like this. He was young and his people needed him.

"But what about a king?" pleaded Jova. "I have come all this way on a quest for a new king. What will our people do?"

"Yes," said Prince Kaboo, the old smile returning fully, "they *do* need a new king, and you are just the one to take them one. My Father told me you are to go back and take King Jesus to them. He is the One they really need. I was preparing to do it myself, but . . . I will not be making the journey."

Jova had heard about Jesus from the missionaries in Monrovia. He had heard about Him from the ship captain and Stephen Merritt in New York. And now, here at Taylor University, the name of Jesus came up often. But no one had clearly explained to him who this Jesus was. So how could he take Him back to Africa to be King?

"I have heard of this Jesus, but who is He?" he asked bluntly.

Kaboo nodded his head slowly in understanding. "You have not heard the good news of the Gospel. Well, I will tell you." The young prince's eyes grew bright.

"God, our Father in heaven, is the Creator of all things. He made the earth, the sky, all life, and every human being. He is only good, but, as you know, people do bad things. They hurt each other. They go to war.

"This makes our Father very sad. He is sad not only because we hurt one another and make our lives miserable but because, in doing bad things, we separate ourselves from Him and His goodness. But our Father loves us so much that He wanted to rescue us from this evil."

Kaboo looked intensely at Jova and continued. "How do we try to make something right when someone has done a very bad thing?" he asked.

Frowning, Jova thought hard. "I don't know. I guess we make them pay for it."

"Give me an example," urged Kaboo.

Jova thought some more. "Well, like the Grebos. When they attack and kill our people, we make them pay to settle the score . . . if we can."

"Exactly. But does that ever solve anything? Is the score ever really settled?"

"No," admitted Jova. "They get mad and attack us back again."

"But what if someone else paid for their evil, someone who was completely innocent?"

Jova had never thought of that idea. "No one is so good as that. Even we Kru people do evil sometimes."

"You are right. You would need someone perfect. God is perfectly good, and so is His Son, Jesus Christ. God sent Jesus from heaven down to earth to pay the price for all our evil deeds. Jesus came to live on earth long, long ago. But we killed Him and did not want to hear His message of God's love."

"The Kru people killed God's Son?" asked Jova in astonishment. He had never heard such a story.

"It wasn't just the Kru people. All people had a

part in killing Him because we are all evil.

"Now this is the great mystery," Kaboo went on, his eyes shining as he leaned forward in his bed. "God said that if we would believe that it was really His Son who came to die in our place, He would forgive us, and the score would be settled. That's the Gospel."

"That's it?" asked Jova, surprised that it was so simple.

"Yes. God has promised that if we believe that He sent Jesus to save us from our sins, we will be forgiven. Then we become God's children and He our Father. And Jesus is our Brother and King."

Jova thought for a moment, then cocked his head to the side as he phrased his question. "But how do we know that Jesus was God's Son? That's a big thing to say, but where is the proof?"

"You ask a good question, but there is an even better answer, one that will amaze you as it has amazed people for ages. We know that Jesus was God's Son, because God raised Him from the dead. Jesus was buried in the ground for three days, but then God brought Him back to life."

"He was moving around, walking, breathing, speaking?"

"Yes, and hundreds of people saw Him. It says so in the Bible."

"That's . . . that's a real miracle! He must be a wonderful King," Jova said, slowly nodding his head as he accepted his prince's report. Then he asked another question. "But how can making Jesus our

King stop the war with the Grebos? What if they don't believe?"

"It would be good," said Kaboo, "if the Grebos believed—and we should tell them about Jesus—but even if they don't believe, we don't have to continue the war. If God has forgiven us because Jesus paid the price for our evil, then we can forgive the Grebos because Jesus paid the price for their evil, too. We don't have to try to get even. Jesus has settled the score."

Jova's head was swimming. "This is all so new," he said faintly.

"I know it is. Just kneel down here by my bed and let me pray for you that God's Spirit would open your mind and help you believe."

Jova knelt down, and Kaboo put his hand on Jova's shoulder and began talking to his Father. As Jova listened, he, too, wanted to be able to call God "Father" and thank Him for sending Jesus.

When he mentioned this desire to Kaboo, Kaboo clapped his hands and said, "Then you *do* believe. Of course you can talk to God. Tell *Him* you believe. Give Him thanks. Say whatever you want to say. He is your Father now, too."

It was so simple . . . but very real.

Some time later, Jova stood up and with a smile of joy on his face said, "Now, together we can go back to our people. You can be their king and we can tell them about Jesus Christ."

Kaboo shook his head. "You do not understand," he explained. "I am dying, so I cannot go with you. I prayed long and hard for our people, and your coming is the answer to my prayer. They do not need me as king. They need Jesus as their King. You must do what I cannot do and go tell them."

"But . . . I cannot. I am too young."

"You came all this way on a quest to become a man. Now is your chance."

"But I do not understand everything about Jesus. I have only just now asked Him to save me. You have been here studying. I will need help."

"Then ask our Father for help, but first promise me that you will go back and take home King Jesus."

Jova felt weak. How could he accomplish such a great task? But as he looked into Kaboo's steady eyes, he nodded. "I promise," he whispered.

The next morning, Jova was helping Professor Stemen mow his front lawn directly across the street from St. Joseph Hospital when they heard a voice calling them. They looked up and saw Kaboo waving from the window of his hospital room. "Don't work him too hard, Professor Stemen!" he called.

Professor Stemen laughed and waved back. "I was just showing Jova how to use this machine," he called up to Kaboo.

"It's better than a dozen goats," called Jova, grinning. "And it leaves no messes."

They all laughed as Kaboo withdrew from the open window.

A few minutes later, one of the nurses hurried out of the hospital and ran over to Jova and Professor Stemen. "You'd better come," she said urgently. "Sammy has just had a sudden relapse."

Jova followed on Professor Stemen's heels as they ran into the hospital and up to Kaboo's room. They stopped at the door. Kaboo lay still on his bed with a peaceful expression on his face. His Bible was open by his side, but he was dead.

On May 12, 1893, at the age of twenty-one, Prince Kaboo, known in America as Samuel Morris, had gone home to his heavenly Father.

The funeral for Samuel Morris was held at the Berry Street Methodist Church where he had been a member. So many people came that hundreds had to stand out in the street.

During the service, the minister asked Jova to say a few words.

As he stepped forward to speak in his broken English, the number of strange people facing him seemed uncountable, but Jova did not lose courage as he spoke in a clear voice.

"I am going back to my Kru people," he said. "The young man you knew as Samuel Morris was Prince Kaboo to me, the only son of our old and dying king. I came to bring Kaboo back because our people need a new king. Now Kaboo cannot go with me because he has gone to his Father in Heaven."

Jova stopped as a sob gripped his throat. Then he continued. "So, I promised Prince Kaboo that I would take King Jesus back to our people. But I need help. I cannot read the Bible. I do not understand very much about the Gospel. But, when I talked to my Father in heaven—to Kaboo's Father and your Father—He told me to ask you. So, I am asking: who will come with me?"

There was a long silence. And then, first one . . . and then another . . . and then another student stood up and said, "I will go with you." Soon, several stu-

dents had volunteered to go as missionaries to Africa to do the work that their beloved classmate had not been able to finish.

After the funeral, Jova walked near the head of the procession to Lindenwood Cemetery where Kaboo was to be buried. Later, Professor Stemen told him that the long parade of people who followed was the largest the Fort Wayne cemetery had ever seen. And even more people lined the streets through which they moved.

With tears in his eyes and thoughts of Prince Kaboo swirling in his mind, Jova looked up from the cobblestones in the street. Without realizing it, his eyes focused on two African men standing on the curb. One was tall and partially bald. The other was short with a bowler hat. Both had three scars on their right cheeks.

Shock sucked the breath out of Jova, and he felt dizzy. He blinked, hoping his mind was playing a trick on him. But the men didn't go away. They were grinning at him—an evil, triumphant grin. How they had found their way to Fort Wayne, Indiana, Jova could not imagine, but there they were—confident that they had won. Prince Kaboo was dead and would not return to Africa to claim his father's throne.

But had they won?

Jova stared at them as he slowly moved along with the funeral procession. No. A quiet confidence settled on him. His quest was a success. He was returning to his people with a new king. He was bringing them King Jesus!

More About Samuel Morris

PRINCE KABOO, later called Samuel Morris, was born in 1872 in the West African country of Liberia. His father was king of his Kru tribe at a time when there was ongoing warfare with the neighboring Grebos.

Being a king in this part of Africa did not mean being the ruler of a whole country or even of all the people of a specific tribe. Kaboo's father was probably the ruler of a large village or possibly several villages in one region. There were undoubtedly other Kru kings in other parts of Liberia. And no single monarch united all the Kru people.

In the whole country, the Kru people far outnumbered the Grebos, but in the region where Kaboo lived, the Grebos had repeatedly defeated his people.

When a defeated king could not pay the war taxes, it was common to surrender someone the king valued in "pawn" until the debt could be paid. This happened the first time with Kaboo when he was a small child, and his father was able to redeem him rather quickly. However, when he was a young adolescent, war broke out again. His people were defeated, and he was placed in pawn a second time. That provides the occasion for the beginning of this story.

This time, Kaboo's father was unable to pay his ransom, and it appears that the Grebos, intent on crushing the Krus forever, kept raising the price.

Kaboo's imprisonment and miraculous escape—including the blinding light and voice from heaven—are recorded in more than one biographical source. In addition to Kaboo's report to missionaries in Monrovia (and later to Dr. T. C. Reade, president of Taylor University), there was at least one other eyewitness. Another young Kru, later named Henry O'Neil or Henry O. Neil, was a slave in the Grebo village. He also saw the light and heard the voice that freed Kaboo. He did not, however, as this book fictionalizes, follow Kaboo through the jungle and witness the nightly guiding light.

A few years later when Henry O'Neil came to Monrovia, he confirmed to missionaries the miracle of Kaboo's release. And in 1892 when Kaboo was a student at Taylor University, he arranged to raise money to bring Henry O'Neil to the United States to receive ministerial training.

Following Kaboo's arrival at the mission station in Monrovia, there were many witnesses to the remarkable deeds of faith that thereafter accompanied his life.

He talked his way onto a sailing ship bound for New York in order to go to America to study God's Word and learn more about the Holy Spirit. The ship was full of cutthroat sailors who hated him as a black person and were just as eager to do each other in. But Sammy (he had taken on a new name by this time) not only intervened to make peace on board the ship but won their friendship, prayed for healing from their diseases, and led most of the crew to the Lord.

In New York, Sammy brought revival to Stephen Merritt's mission and to various local churches in which he preached.

At Taylor University, he did much the same. Soon the newspapers were carrying reports of this remarkable African young man who was instigating revival wherever he went—on the campus, in the local churches of Fort Wayne, and even in revival meetings conducted in such public places as a roller-skating rink.

In the winter of 1892–1893, the school was nearly ready to close its doors for lack of funds to pay its bills. But Sammy Morris's example of faith not only made him a leader among his fellow students, but inspired a discouraged faculty and administration. The board of trustees decided to use the Samuel Morris Faith Fund to raise enough money to move the school from Fort Wayne to Upland, Indiana. It was just the thing to preserve the university.

And though Samuel's death seemed like an untimely tragedy, God used it to inspire a substantial number of Taylor students to go to the mission field, many to Africa in Sammy's stead. There was even a Taylor University Bible School established in Africa.

But perhaps the most typical tribute to Prince Kaboo was paid by the captain of the tramp ship on which Sammy came to New York. When he learned that Sammy had died on May 12, 1893, he was so overcome with emotion that he could not speak for some time. Then he said that most of the old crew were still on board and eager to find out about their beloved hero and minister. After all, he had changed life on that ship. Before he came aboard, no one had ever prayed out loud, but after Sammy shared the Gospel with them, they became like one family—a family that could talk to their Father.

For Further Reading

Baldwin, Lindley. *Samuel Morris.* Minneapolis, Minn.: Bethany House Publishers, 1942.

Evans, A. R. *Sammy Morris.* Grand Rapids, Mich.: Zondervan Publishing House, 1958.

Konkel, Wilbur. *Jungle Gold: The Amazing Story of Sammy Morris.* London: Pillar of Fire Press, 1966.

Masa, Jorge O. *The Angel in Ebony.* Upland, Ind.: Taylor University Press, 1928.

Reade, Thaddeus C. *Samuel Morris.* Upland, Ind.: Taylor University, 1896.

Stocker, Fern Neal. *Sammy Morris.* Chicago: Moody Press, 1986.